GROSS INTRUSION
and Other Stories

By the same author

The Fall of the House of Usher by Edgar Allan Poe, a play adaptation by Steven Berkoff (Wikor Drama Library No. 47, The Netherlands, 1975)

East (Agamemnon and *The Fall of the House of Usher)*

Metamorphosis (adapted from Kafka) and *Three Theatre Manifestos* (in *Gambit 32)*

GROSS INTRUSION
and Other Stories

by

Steven Berkoff

JOHN CALDER . LONDON
RIVERRUN PRESS . DALLAS

First published in Great Britain 1979
by John Calder (Publishers) Ltd.,
18 Brewer Street, London W1R 4AS

First published in the USA 1979
by riverrun press Inc.,
4951 Top Line Drive,
Dallas, Texas 75247

ISBN 0 7145 3685 7 casebound

Printed by M. & A. Thomson Litho Ltd., East Kilbride
Bound by Hunter & Foulis Ltd., Edinburgh

CONTENTS

Acknowledgements

'Say a Prayer for Me' was first published in *New Writing and Writers 13* in 1976

FOR SHELLEY

Say a Prayer for Me

The manifestation of his lust was the salute to heaven by his obedient 'Lieutenant Flesh', whenever Doris genuflected with bucket and brush and paid homage to the dirty floor with bubbly warm suds... her generous ass rising and falling majestically as she pushed the brush forwards and backwards never failed to rouse the sweetest arias in the secret parts of Harry's anatomy and he would pause on the way to eggs and bacon floating in lavas of grease which fuelled him for yet another day in M. Burton bespoke tailor and outfitter ... Doris's curly hair springing off the nape particularly attracted his base carnal throb, the sight of her white revealed flesh beneath the hair ... how the nape was a delicious ingot of pleasure ... that small rivulet and delicate avenue. But he never paused long enough to cough a word of carefully rehearsed, 'Hallo Dot, coming up to my room for a sensitive communication between two socialist vegetarians with sensualist leanings,' but such pithy utterances were not to drop from his anxious and mellifluous lips ... his passion was too strong and faltered trembling against failure ... the endlessly long days in the store standing on his arches that were breaking under the dead weight that unrelieved boredom inflicts on a live body ... each evening washing the collar and cuffs of his shirt so that it should be dry for the following morning (possessing only two white shirts, the mandatory uniform made that little ritual necessary) or forgetting, he'd shrewdly put talcum powder on the collar and cuffs instead. This method though practical, caused quicker dirtying and faster fraying and consequently more frequent scrubbing. He would welcome the customers who were as confused about their clothes as he was about his whole life, hence they went to cheap multiple stores ... hoping to hide themselves in the wholesale taste of others, in the latest three button suit with insert pockets and Prince of Wales check, not varying too greatly from last year's model to cause any crisis of orientation. They sought in those infinite varieties of drab grey and lovat the answer to many puzzling features of their lives, most of all the key that would unlock their disturbing mediocrity ... the wife would stand in front of her man who suddenly became a sheepish object with no faculty of taste or choice ... suddenly was granted to the woman infallible depths of judgment and knowledge ... while the male seemingly had been made impotent by the metal edge of the tape measure stabbing his crutch. Unwholesome indignity 'would you please open your legs sir!' ... try desperately not to get too close and be made to feel their sagging equipment as his finger and thumb gingerly held the end of the metal extension. Harry, whilst dreaming about playing Petruchio or Richard II (out of work actor filling in as temporary labour) would reel at the stench, acrid ... bitter, emanating from the evacuating areas of some Irish labourer or Indian who for indigenous reasons smelt somewhat higher than Harry and he would bite back the vomit in his throat ... during the long hours in the shop, he mentally ran through all the plays he'd ever performed ... play over the good nights and gloss

over the bad ones . . . the bravos for one
performance that he was so especially good in . . . he
played a weak snivelling psychopath and was
thought good in the role but an actress who wasn't
disposed towards him claimed that he was only
playing himself, and advanced the same notion to
the company who started to share her view when he
failed miserably to make his mark in other roles.
Only Harry was convinced that her judgment was
untrue . . . he was good in that role, the local critics
said so; 'rare observation' they said. He liked that
word 'rare', mulled over that review whenever he
was depressed, made him feel good . . . so what, if he
suffered the stinking effluvium of their dirty
unbathed bodies, Harry was rare, and he would one
day show them how rare he was . . . he'd then
remember all the Directors he ever worked for, who
for some reason never called him anymore . . . his
first nights and last ones and the little parties after in
the dressing rooms . . . the nights he'd sweat blood
and fear and for no particular reason sail through on
another night. The nights his friends came
and chomped; his successes with his mouth in the
bar warmed by the whisky that he also bought for
everyone . . . 'Well done Harry . . . you were superb
dear,' while he bought everyone's meal, just for
liking him . . . That was enough. I'll pay, I'm good.
I'm up there on the green . . . I got through another
night in paroxysms of fear . . . (secretly little spies in
his subconscious delivered messages to him that he
would try to reject . . . messages that spelt fear,
'failure, forget your lines! You're a bum . . . you're
good . . . sometimes but mostly you're a fake who's
afraid of first nights and throws them for the rest of
the cast who bail you out' . . . 'but I wasn't always like
that,' he shrieks at those canny little spies . . . 'your
hair's getting thin' (true so I'll wear a toupé, so what,

they're undetectable these days, my friend Bruce has got one, he can even swim in it) ... other times but usually not unconnected with alcohol ... 'you're a genius Harry, so observant, so "rare" ... so strong ... you're another Olivier') ... 'yes sir, 3 button and side vents' said Hamlet, Richard II ... Othello ... the fire in his soul that ignited those immortal creatures was crushed under the daily barrage of shit that stayed hard, constipated and adhered to the bowels of his spirit like concrete ... he could willingly tear the smug face off this or that man, could, 'tear him all to pieces, ... were every hair upon his head a life, there would not be enough to satisfy my revenge,' he'd misquote. The Manager would watch him curiously, unaware of those monumental dramas raging inside Harry's skull. Like those people who with earphones are surrounded by a deafening cacophony revealing nothing to the onlooker except a distant glazed look, thus it was with H. The Manager tolerated these temporary theatricals, but disliked them for their chameleon-like ease in changing their lives ... for being able to essentially grasp in a week that which he had spent 30 boring, empty, fruitless wasted years doing, until the sacrifice of his youth was the reward of the Managership of a fading and ailing branch of M. Burton, a branch that even unbeknown to him was shortly to be lopped off at its withered stump with the Manager still clinging to it while singing of the virtues of bespoke. To build up the importance of the trade the Manager had alluded to H the complexities of the work. The difficulties of measuring, the subtleties of serving ... nefarious and discreet ways of licking asses and inducing emotional black-mail by making the creeps buy out of guilt ... buy what they couldn't afford ... harrassing the customers for your threadbare tot of commission (these very methods had no doubt led to the eventual cancer of that branch, since word gets round in poor areas). 'Go forward No. 3,' the Manager would bark as a pale innocent customer would shabbily slink in, 'yes sir, what can I do for you sir!' Harry would screech at some nervous Cypriot, making an impression of rancid keeness for the Manager's watering thin stare. 'Forward No. 3.' H had metamorphosed from 'there cracks a noble heart' ... to sticky ... unshaved ... chafed grubby talced cuffs, fallen arches No. 3, with soiled underwear ... the direct inheritance of being womanless and sapped of all being, of all confidence ... all joy, no man but a pest. A pest that needs to eat! A bug! Why live fool! Habit. He answered the question himself. 'Patch pockets, Donegal Tweed, Centre Vent' ... only for the freedom when he erupts from the store like a fart. And he thinks of Doris, the scrubber in his digs, his bed and breakfast for working men. Plump Doris bending to scrub the dusty torn lino, the house cleaner. Nice Doris. The vision in Harry's head, the 'perhaps this time I'll speak, if she's washing in the kitchen.' He did. The day had been too strong in horror and had seared open some chemicals that had spelt a drop of courage to his failing spirit. That night after washing his collar and cuffs he came upon her on the stairs as she was about to leave and inferred in jolly tones all casual like with plenty of heart-thump how nice to see her after hours so to speak to which she easily and pleasantly accorded. 'That was easy, what a surprise' ... she would pop in the next night after supper (bed, breakfast and evening meals), he shared a lodging house with other lonely ageing unmarried men in an area of London half way between hell and purgatory. In the evenings they sat in a cold room watching TV but knew, these womanless blokes that the flickering box of smiling faced comperes of quiz shows and the like would only postpone the sense of death which crept on them as surely compounded by that box as by the dinner squirming inside them which could only have been made with indifference crossed with venom . . . but this night Harry would enter the Elysian Fields . . . would congress with Aphrodite and Juno, would *live* for once . . . she'll come up after she's washed the supper dishes . . . Oh fortunate hero . . . servant of Priapus, upon thy white steed will he fly far from M. Burton and No. 3, float serenely into remote and profane regions of delirious escape . . . my angel Doris's ass leaping heavenward with her pussy, Xmas wrapped in pink nylon, (brief glimpses last week) would sneak, ogre of wobbling carnal appetites, into his room and be impaled by H. He would live again, . . . enter not Burtons, but through his menacing, twitching itching, pink, stiff, arched cock that he would swift into her . . . into that steaming cauldron of Doris . . . 'Oh hell and fuck!' As he sprints upstairs to wash his equipment and waited with thumping ventricles, and fag choked minutes later . . . a knock on his door . . . delicate . . . like a whisper. . . then came an unwelcome visitor – fear . . . 'Oh Christ', like the fear of those first nights it entered even here as if starved of attention all this time it had waited for something important enough to Harry that would swell his arteries with the blood needed for a gesture of life and the black phantom of fear descended greedily to syphon it off. 'Oh God' . . . he feebly invoked . . . he tried to smash it out of his skull but the images he had made of the future died . . . the myriad paintings his skull had produced in its gallery faded as if washed with torrential rain. He opened the door with fear clinging to him still, like an invisible incubus fastened to his jugular vein.

There she was ... cherubic with rosy rubric cheeks and glinting eyes ... she was wholesomely flushed with expectancy . . . her *expectancy*. 'I can't stay long,' she smiled nervously ... while his salient or selling point was diminishing by the over-keenness of his love and the anticipation of her wants. His whorish picture of her genuflecting, 'easy grubby scrubber' was replaced by sturdy, strong, upright, made-up, expectant Doris . . . she seemed to grow as he had been diminishing ... he satiated the porny area of his brain with a succession of tatty, threadbare pictures of her knees bent onto the mat and her creamy ass and vale to recoup the blood to that part nature demands for her deeds. But these days blood mostly rushed to his face in sweaty humiliation for his soul's sacrifice at Burton's and he cannot fuck with his face. And now again his face received the homage of blood that was meant for his prick. He wondered why and what had become of that bursting impatient tumescence that had twisted him up in desire until at last he had unfastened his strangled vocal chords to speak to her. She sat on the bed and he with fag relaxed just enough to act out a clumsy gesture of sexual greed. Sensed he an awful and sad need to prove his worth and her attractiveness, little knowing that she would have been just as happy for a chat ... to break the equally relentless monotony of her own plight ... her threadbare daily existence with child at home, this unmarried gentle Doris saw in Harry a scintilla of sensitive being and hoped that what she believed she saw in him would also see the same in her. Might have detected in her the images of softness, homeliness, wifeliness and motherhood. Sure, he would understand her little two year old at home with mum ... would like her, she hoped, smelling as she did of flour and fresh apples ... she could look after him ... Had seen and recognised the ravages of neglect that she was keen to mend. She had liked his voice (how the lonely look for virtues) a voice broader and different to the other tenants ... gentle brown eyes. Thought that in him she would find the redemption she sought. Had her prayers eventually come true, that she uttered nightly to the blessed Holy Virgin ... Had in Harry, soft, pliant baritone shy Harry she found the man she needed in her guts, to protect, comfort and sew for. She thought so ... she needed to. She carefully made up and thought that even if he wanted to fuck her on the first night perhaps he would see her again ... this one would, since she was afraid she lacked enough interest in her being to possess a man for long enough without succumbing to his blackmailing desire or anger if the passion she aroused was not immediately assuaged ... so with Harry she was prepared to take this risk, just one more time ... but trusting somehow in her prayers that he would succumb to the needs of real love and would be enchanted by her. And in this spirit thus she rapped on the door as gently as a caress; and thus in fear and self-loathing did Harry answer it. Fear bred from a fast depreciating assessment of his own worth. Doth reality ever live up to the private scenarios of hope? Not in Harry's case ... they mustn't ... they cannot be allowed to challenge those scenarios since that would be setting one's dreams against the scope of his endeavour. And this endeavour was already weakened by fighting on other fronts. He grabs her in a rehearsed gesture which hurts her as much as it betrays him ... surely goodness and mercy is what is called for here ... stroke the curve of cheek ... kiss the curls on her nape ... hold her palm in yours and confess in tears your frailty and beg absolution ... let the soul stride out of the body in all its lights ... ignite her spirit ... cradle her hopes like the Holy Ghost ... cry unto the lord for thanks ... and render unto Caesar that which is Caesar's ... feel her heavy tears from the melting ice of anguish that you dissolve, feel them cascading down your face. And let the angels of libido feast only after the benedictions of Aphrodite ... sing Gloria and Kyrie Eleison ... 'the heavens break open.' ... But Harry dimly aware of these injunctions to his soul pulled back ... smoked a fag which she shared and sent differing prayers to darker beings for the parole of his cock ... desperate transactions were going on at infernal depths whose conclusions were to be even greater fetters ... he relaxed a little ... not much ... enough to feed a kitten (the loan was coming through) a bare splinter of feeling threaded its bloody course and he fumbled with her clothes against her feeble cries and disappointments ... the devil flashed some tawdry pictures to enliven him ... just enough ... was made to think of her bending down, humiliated and scrubbing, focusing on her innocent display of torn underwear ... Ah! Would this match with what he felt, what he could relate to, in fact to what *he* was. Was her sturdy uncompromising and hopeful glance as she entered the room too healthy for this withered plant. So he turned her over in imitation of those postcard pictures and attempted to fuck this creature who was just an article of flesh and clothing ... Faceless, in the sad poor furniture of his mind, pushed and heaved; her crying but yielding ... losing even now the gentle pictures she hitherto had formed ... losing them and fearing them lost for ever, while his deformed cartoons gained ascendancy ... yet the optimism that perpetuated the human race, that gives aid to the dying, that raises even that slashed wounded bull to its feet for its last futile clumsy charge, that will never say die even on the point of death, that will attempt to revoke the irrevocable . . . inspired her sufficiently to hope that even after this initial degradation, born she thought out of a confusion of passion, frustration and filth would lead in a time of repose, to her cuddling him in her arms and forgiving him for being taken so cheaply. But now she couldn't even see his face but endured her wet cheeks on his rather grimy pillow . . . during this onslaught, if it can be called that . . . while Harry had taken a loan off Priapus against heavy interest (a further diminishing of his confidence) he hoped to fulfil his slender ambition of merely filling her space for the duration of time it takes to be a bed-sitter hero. This was another night he would 'get through' not savour or enjoy but endure to the final act, when the audience would go to their homes forgetting in a short while that he ever lived or breathed. Only the devil knew since the devil and its mate death feed upon a vacuum and lie in wait . . . for them Harry and his like were important people that fed their monstrous and gloating appetites . . . the strong only throw them crumbs but Harry donates his whole body . . . even so they were tiring of him . . . Harry meanwhile was performing his ritual 'in and out' albeit a trifle limply but still at least making the gesture, when he started to think of the shop, perhaps seeing the shirt hanging over the chair as he was mounting her made a small mental reminder to him to wash the cuffs that night . . . how the soul of man is distracted when not committed . . . to think of the shirt cuffs *now* when inside poor Doris who was pushing her ample bum in the air to satisfy this beast's need to take his victims from behind . . . OOOh! No! No! That shirt took his cock from his mind – that shirt hanging there like he was in it with its worn cuffs finally snuffed the hypocrisy that had filled his penis; that amazing construction of millions of years of evolutionary miracles had in Harry become uncertain, vulnerable. Not unquenchable, unbeatable, infallible as are nature's laws, but the appendage to his sense of failure. He failed Doris, he failed himself, and he failed God, he failed fate that had brought them together, and he failed her two year old that he surely would have loved, and his cock dismally fell out with a 'slurp' ... he mumbled something about 'being tired', 'sorry' 'not feeling too well' ... 'wonder what could be wrong?' ... Doris ... simple in understanding the jigsaws and circumambulations of human nature interpreted this in her own way – she was plain, not unwholesome, but not very attractive in the standard way of prettiness that men like ... not attractive enough even for a first fuck that she hoped might bring them to a closer union of heart, on her knees and elbows stimulating the morning's denigration with the evening's defilement. Both had souls that if united would have conquered everything ... worse ways loneliness. After comes strength. Her baby needs a father ... this man needs her ... instead, her weeping, him angry and helpless staring at that shirt like some foul intruder had entered the room ... 'who are you pale stranger? ... OUT!' he said to her, ... 'Fine, Oh ... see you tomorrow' ... she said, 'sorry' she actually apologised (did crowds of angels sing her to sleep?). The door closed gently and Harry went about scrubbing the sleeves of his shirt.

Master of Café Society

Up he would get as soon as dawn broke ... the day tracking over the slatey roofed house like cracked ice and glinting sprays and thin shafts of sun-white ... birds sang and sparrows crescendoed in triplets and arpeggios ... the sheets pulled back, feet out, toes wriggling, expectation rising, nose stuffed, phlegm sucked into the back of the throat, gathered into the mouth like a green harvest and then fed into a virgin Kleenex ... crushed, plop into basket. Outside engines beginning to throat up . . . RARARARARARA ... Doors open and slam into the new dawn of life ... each new day indeed a miracle thawing out ... the world has made yet another revolution and still tracks through space holding a tight link to the everlasting sun whose gentle heat will not abide; the seas remain in the sea and do not flood the land; the nuclear devastation has not happened yet as promised, and no earthquakes disturb our shores. Revolution will not claim millions of lives here and we will not starve today, no fear of famine; the poles will not melt through overheating by an atmosphere already thickened with a layer of carbon monoxide that will act as a magnifying agent to the sun's rays, not today anyway. I will not die today of cancer nor be brutally stabbed in the throat by an irate black panther choosing me to avenge some other deadly feud, no.

21

So as the grey clouds stole across H's roof like a sargasso sea and as H carefully made his bachelor bed tucking in the coverlet, he prepared his mind to the joys of breakfast:—

The master of the working man's café society.

Steadfastly holding the same stretch of road each day, his perennial ritual, (the same stomp down the road, so why don't you bloody say so), his eyes glazing already at the too familiar sight on the horizon, blurring against the dreadful sameness, and wishing for fronds and palm trees and blistered chairs sun-baked and creaking under an Aegean sky, hot white islands, domestica wine and fat round sleepy tomatoes, but, as the unchanging sun rises with bloody and bulging cheek to penetrate the cool and fragrant mystery of dawn so doth rise Harry, phlegm-soaked and blinking and as it sinks again with the dusk each evening without fail trailing garlands of purple glory, H will be there, wondering at the mystery of the universe as he contemplates yet another empty day ripped off the few petals of his life.

The image of breakfast floated before him like a menu visualised by computers and fed into his brain.

Hunger I like/it gives me a sense of purpose/for fuck's sake you can't live like this all your life/I eat to give myself a reason/I arise like all the other workers/buy a paper/sit down/they think I'm working/who else gets up to eat at 8 am looking tired/and yes I can see the real workers 'cause they're always talking about work/fuck it I work in my head/don't you stare at.me like that in your slave's uniform/your paint splashed overalls/work doesn't grow on trees. **MOTHER** *. . . some actors worse than you I've seen on T.V. Ii makes me sick I mean with your looks like Paul Newman you look!!!!*

H had the same breakfast every morning. Why change? When he changed it confused him. It broke the perfect order of things. It took too long to decide whether one dish was better than another, but since breakfast was the one special time of normality, getting up early, washing, being like all the other workers who were preparing themselves to enter the morning still freckled with white thick cups, sandwich toasted and packed full, eat slowly let the first corner explode taste sensations in the mouth and hold back from rushing, since after this breakfast you are bequeathed purgatory, until once again hunger calibrates the day with purpose...

H carefully opens the paper at the theatre reviews. Oh Ho! 'X's play is dull but sharp performances from the actors,'...lousy actors always flog their mechanical characters on TV which buy up their little stockpile of samey parts, so and so plays such and such.

'We're looking for a statuesque young actress who can play between 20 and 45 ...'

'Oh, I have just the person ...'

'Oh super ...'

'I don't like to offer it to you darling, since I wish it were bigger ...'

'Oh no, I'd really love to do it.'

'You are kind but do look at the script first and let me know.'

'O.K. darling but it looks fun.'

'Thought you were super last week in the final episode of *Justine* by the Marquis De Sade.'

'Gosh that was exhausting.'

'I can imagine . . . bye bye ducky. I'll discuss money with your agent.'

CHORUS OF FAMILY: *These actors would convince the backside of my ass too good for them/Shmutters/No feeling/Not an ounce/'Cause you're too good for them/Don't worry one day you'll show them/You'll have them licking your . . . your agent doesn't ring you . . . /So when are you going to get married/You're getting on for . . . Soon you will be . . . God don't tell me how old I am. I bury myself in the dust bin of wasted days and vomit my heart out and sit on the 73 bus sweating upstairs as the bus stands in the middle of Oxford Street and look how little I can do/And who lives for the sight of me/Gagged inside my raw mouth/I eat my failure like acid/Scorching/Hold back my tears . . . and scorn my mother but I bite into her nipples withered and ancient as an old sack . . . I bite into her . . . take her by the throat and make her eyes bulge/After this I set her down gently and make a cup of tea/Dad's watching TV all the time and didn't see a thing/He was stuck to the screen as a fly to paper/I will kill all the first born theatrical agents/DAD: How come you don't get more TV/I saw a part you could have played on your head/Don't drink to get to sleep/Help! That's no good Harry . . . MUM: My life you should have been a dancer so graceful you are . . . Isn't he, Dad . . . DAD: What did you say? MUM: Graceful Harry is, I said he's so graceful that when he acts it's like watching a dancer, I said . . . DAD: He's an actor not a dancer . . . he acts like an actor/not a dancer/I opened his trousers . . . I opened my father's trousers and saw his 70 year old penis and it resembled mine except his was only slightly withered/and pulled his y-fronts down, old and faded but clean and dad said 'son you could be a good actor you're a professional/don't do it son'/but I took his withered old gentle cock in my hands and waited/I myself had made a journey through that very same place/mother smiling uncertainly as if trying to recall the time/we waited patiently and sure enough after a few minutes I*

*detected a few thin strands of life stretching
themselves out into affirmation/there's life in the
old boy yet/well done dad/we all celebrated with a
cup of tea.*

Some Cafés have a personality all of their own and H
would sit in this one for the duration of the sandwich
and order a second cup of tea ... Oh dear ... the
sandwich has gone, diminished to a fast receding
dream, it rests intestinally bright ... but the second
cup of tea will start a second ritual ... a fresh cup ...
we can begin all over again ... the workers graze past
the windows and the cars form themselves into
caterpillars. The traffic thickens and slows down
and H can clearly see their eyes staring dumbly to the
side from their fat satiated breakfasted faces. The
snail's pace causes them insecurity and they no
longer face the front, necessary with speed since all
they have to view is the standing back of another car.
So they peer out of the corner of their eyes with a
slothful curiosity, the way pigs raise their heads
from the swill when disturbed ... the world that
morning had been making itself into a stew and H
sipped his second cup ... purpose would soon dry up
with the absorbtion of it. He reads the paper ...
soaks up politics/theatre/ballet/history/literature/
sport/crime/sex/murder/tits/gags/gossip/fashion/
films/painting and nature ... and folds it up ... it is
nearly over ... the breakfast extinguished, the bed
made, the walk achieved, the selection of café
decided on, the food ordered, the table chosen ... the
position of ass ascertained, first tea drunk, sky
surveyed and the wonders of the universe wondered
about, thoughts collected, choice chosen, face
shaved. There is no more, an event that collects your
life into a ritual has come to an end: you could make
another ritual, but no. Hunger has been blunted ...

the body fuelled for work, attainment, achievement, risk, effort, courage, daring responsibility. You stride out of the cafe . . . alive . . . paying the bill with the certainty of a man about to embark on the serious business of holding your fragment of the world together . . . the manager smiles at your determined exit, admiring those secret events in your life that make you an important personage, in his eyes.

Your cousin Willy is so wealthy now . . . /he runs a Rolls Royce/doing so well . . . what did he do I ask myself/he married well/of course he did/before that he was nothing/Aunty Betty saw you the other night on the telly/ as the astronaut/ could tell it was you in spite of the helmet/and she rang Willy to tell him to watch it/you know, he's very fond of you/you should go down and see him/but he wasn't in and when she got back you were off the screen/what a shame but she liked the bit she . . . no your father can't work anymore but we'll manage/don't you worry/social security/so who's asking you for money/when you've got it I know you'll give/I know that/hold on a moment son your father wants to talk to you/hallo son, I thought you did that part smashin'/you looked the image of Paul Newman/ don't worry about money/listen I'd rather starve alive with your mother and feed on rats than take a penny from you that you might need for make-up etc.

H strolled down the street, his conscription with the workers of the world was at an end, his brief march with the hordes had come to a halt and now he must turn back, no longer striding along in the bright dewey sunlight with cloth cap and sandwich box, ruddy cheeks, illumined with the glow of purpose, tool-box gripped in the fist and the thought of horizons to be conquered, wood that needs to be shaped and hewn, metal smelted, back bending under an easy load for a fit body and a mate's rough voice shouting instructions ... no bricks to grip and chip to size, no plans to pore over, no sweat to wipe from your brow, no lunch break to look forward to, nor tea time either, no home to rush home to, no dirt or grime to wash off, no woman to say 'My god you're a mess, what have you been doing Harry ... jump in the bath while I get your tea'/*like Paul Newman he looks/with looks like that he could be.../your cousin Willy is doing so well/your father wants a word with you/don't worry son/Rome wasn't built in a day ...*

Harry strolled down the street and opened his familiar front door and re-entered his house as if to say 'what am I doing here'... I should be somewhere else ... he sat down and felt like crying... he sat in the chair and for the life of him did not know what to do ... so he did cry, he cried like a man cries and to see a man cry is not an easy thing to witness, because a man will cry only when the end of the world has come ... he stared out of his swollen eyes when the thought hit him ... 'Fuck it, I forgot to get the cat food.'

Daddy

The steam was rising furiously in clouds that obscured the other bodies in the room. He was watching the figures move in and out of focus like ghosts ... the sweat oozed gratefully down his body and over his eyes and trickled into his mouth ... every pore became an exit for the dirt and grime that was locked inside his skin ... the heat moved everything, shifted and broke up dirt into valleys and streams, and he rubbed his legs and belly, satisfied ... it rolled off in shreds of dead matter ... he was cleaning ... burning up in a slow lather of sweat ... his head rested on a wooden curved block, and the thin apron they issued at the reception lay like a wet Greek toga barely covering over the erogenous zone ... so carefully placed as to reveal to the inquisitive bulging eyes the faintest rotunda of an aware prick ... not stiff yet ... but just lolling expectantly ... a dark shadow in his groin within which fantasies danced and formed mirages in the heads of the old queens that sat close by or walked casually up and down ... they walked as if garlanded in chiffon gowns carrying steaming trains which dissolved behind them ... only the hissing of the vapour and the occasional slap as flesh massaged itself, morse-coding its proximity to the other occupants, were to be heard ... the rest was heavy and expectant silence ... it was hot, becoming unbearable if one moved ... the air scorched into the lungs and hurt, I could leave thought Cyril and take a plunge—icy-cool—and return, but just as he was thinking this he became aware of figures rising and sinking ... one or two leaving ... the patterns in the steam creating new configurations and swirls as the doors opened and shut ... if the door to the outer room stayed shut for a while the steam's thickening camouflage would prevent snooping eyes from detecting what two intense and barely moving figures were doing in the corner ... would only just make out a shape and then one has at least eight to ten feet warning to recover the apron and conceal the monstrous swelling before the eyes came too near ... each figure feared the others as if convinced of the solitariness of their deviation ... scarcely crediting the moving misty creatures with desires as strange as their own ... the separate race, inured and conditioned as odd ... from the early days when the desire to be a woman and want other men was a dirty criminal passion ... so this fear grew into alert caution, even though the occupants of the steam rooms were of a feather ... this fear to be caught in the centre of one's shame, thrown out, or just ashamed of their dirty itch ... like schoolboys jerking each other off in the lav, mustn't be caught by teacher ... and yet fear breeds a stranger thrill at the same time ... to be seen in the heat of one's delight, in the daring exposing of one's secret fantasies ... no one knows ... no one, not one's closest friend, wife, family, not in there, in the sanctuary of heat and steam ... one is depersonalised into mere hard warm pliant flesh ... naked and nameless no names given ... not even speaking ... that is part of the ritual of sacrifice ... the knowledge of the name, the timbre of the voice which would identify or code the speaker would make it

impossible ... would reveal a conscious act ... so no.
I have left my body ... it does things that the owner
of a voice would never do ... only unguarded blood-
filled and aching flesh making its own demands,
being the king for the day ... just the nervous eyes
peering ... the hand moves in slow motion, its
fingers, white tarantula ... crawling nearer and
nearer the source of blood-boiled lust, they halt
nervously ... signal caught by a victim whose knees
crook casually 'accidentally' apart ... reveals the
blood-filled prey ... a tumescent lump of flesh ...
the hand now moves like clawed hunger and seizes
the offering between finger and thumb ... starts to
press, squeeze, rub up and down slowly, gently, with
the confidence of one who knows that ensnared in its
grasp is an animal that cannot escape, entrapped in
the prison of its own terrible desire whose only
freedom lies in the power of the unknown manipu-
lator ... the freedom wll come when his prick will
grow so huge that he will be able to crawl through its
centre ... when his body will simply leave and turn
to lava ... will throb his thick white swill and he will
escape ... escape, metamorphosed into a pool of
spunk that will be washed away along with the
collected sweat and dirt and other emissions of the
baths ... shadows come and go ... the hand stops on
occasion (an alert hind sniffing danger?), figures
dissolve themselves in the swirling mists like beings
brought to life for a few seconds and then returned
to the incorporate air ... the hand continues ...
wanking as only a man knows how to wank another
man ... with the specific and ancient knowledge of
the flash points in that stiff and bursting cock, able
like a guided missile to home in on the areas the
wanker knows so well. Searching the rills and ridges,
the exact amount of pressure ... the time when speed
takes one into incredible flights into the strato-

sphere ... not too soon ... don't spend too fast ... the recomposing shapes in the mist provide insurance against over-eagerness ... the strange warm satisfaction of a man's fist, heavy, large, seeking out one's shame ... that's what's so good about it ... so secretive ... not open, accepted naturally ... meet the folks ... but mysterious ... dirty ... unaccepted ... even by oneself in the cold light of day ... there, clothes describe the owner's taste, class, personality ... too much given away, too much to risk ... only in the steam room protected by the blankets of mist rising and the neutral anonymity of nakedness can you surrender to the full, the implications and impulses the clothed conscious daylight being would reject ... except ... the memory of some fleeting, hurried experiences in cinemas protected by noise and darkness. His teenage was scored by several such events (perhaps the birthplace of his corruption and subsequent desire for darkness and secrecy), as if sewn into his unconscious was the knowledge that male desire and furtiveness were immutable ... the image of his wet prick spraying his pants ... his heavy breathing ... the awkwardness of not being able to stretch his legs or open them to release his high young fulsome jets ... no, here was better ... one can wash the spunk away in the shower ... in the plunge ... wash away the guilt ... not face the brilliant light of day after the cinemas damp sticky gropings ... no words exchanged ... just let the hand ... strong heavy masculine hand work its joys ... and let one's body melt away into the steam ... into the water ... into the drains ... feeling that, he relaxed, and waited ... sensing a shape through the mist that grew larger ... he closed his eyes, partially surrendered like a woman. That's what was so burningly satisfying, being the object of lust, his wife could never do that for

him; make him feel ... coy ... he withdrew a knee ...
make him work for it ... he could act a woman so
well ... as a child he fantasised about being a girl,
who was fucked so hard by so many men ... images
occured of sucking so many juicy hard pricks ... as a
girl he did not imagine that he could exercise the
restraint that women seem so able to assume ... even
when he eventually fucked them ... from where, he
often wondered, grew this strange flower of his
desire ... the offshoot from his natural fucking male
self, often called a womaniser, a ladies' man, a Don
Juan ... where developed this curious thing that
grew like a small delicate unknown ... unclassified
plant within his psyche ... blossoming in those
special seasons within the body and spreading its
noxious fragrant scent through his senses which did
not resist but simply and casually obeyed its strange
demands ... and that particular afternoon taking
time off to feed this flower in the Turkish baths ...
no one knew, or even hazarded the vaguest guess ...
mother ... wife ... father ... no not him, though
from him he sensed the greatest fear ... the greatest
censure of any fault he harboured ... his father was
the governor of a prison and he the prisoner having to
answer for all his sins which seemed engraved on his
forehead. Upright, righteous father ... he even felt
guilty standing before him as if his desire might be
writ in letters of fire ... these thoughts flew between
him and his blood and drained some stiffness from
his member but he immediately washed them away ...
the heat made his mind swim ... its power melted
away any distasteful images before they could
coagulate in his mind ... it purged and purified until
all that was left was body ... naked relaxed and
expectant body ... the air scorched into his lungs
like sulphur ... he could only endure it a few
moments more ... the figure grew out of the mist

and sat near him ... its intention seemed plain ... he dimly saw an arm stealing towards him and he lay back like a cat ready to be stroked ... from a lying down position he need only encounter the hand and could keep an eye on the door ... the strategy was familiar to all ... the stranger's hand found him ... found his flesh ... primed and ready ... and the stranger wanted only his hand and eye to be fed by the younger man's prick ... relinquishing his gaze only to keep surveillance on the door ... if a shadow seemed in that faded moist jungle to linger, attracted by the composition of two still bodies ... the secrets they might harbour ... the stranger's hand would stop, then return, adding by its absence a sharper awareness ... what a strong hand ... how well it sensed the rhythm of his body ... like an organist pulling out the right stops ... fantasies crawled through his eyes and dissolved into a myriad of liquid shapes ... the sperm felt like it was boiling... the stranger's frenzied strokes slowed suddenly ... not wishing his quarry to escape until he lowered his head to receive the warm homage in his mouth ... dangerous, if someone came in the door ... the act of recovery to upright position would reveal their game . . . would be too violent a gesture . . the spunk ready to emit at this point held back, reined in by this sudden conscious act of defence . . . the body wanted now too much . . . too much to care for caution ... the sap was rising on its carefree abandoned voyage to ecstasy ... let him, it will be over soon ... surrender to it ... the stranger leaned over ... his thinning hair revealed a shiny sweaty dome which further decelerated the onslaught to come ... he didn't wish to see him so clearly ... older than he liked, even though he did like older men ... this one seemed too old ... if he sucked hard he may reverse the slowing process ...

the older man looked up as if to query humbly the almost imperceptible, but certainly softening growth in his mouth ... THEIR EYES FOR ONE SECOND IN THAT CHAMBER OF HELL LOCKED ... the mist cleared enough to show ... something ... He was in a dream ... knew he was trapped in a nightmare and struggled to free himself from it ... knew certainly that this nightmare would go, too incredible ... too horrible ... must go ... but his flesh was real ... the marble slab in the room was real ... the heat was real ... the sudden release of the stranger's hand was real ... the standing up and rushing out of the room was also real ... as he pounded up the stairs, and even without showering dressed, still sweating furiously ... out in the cold air ... still sweating even more now than in that inferno ... he swore to himself that the face of his father that lowered itself on to his cock, was a manifestation of his guilt . . . a vision of fear that harboured itself in his brain ... a revenge on his split mind ... the flower seeking to dominate his being... but the balding head, those eyes, the white face that seemed to twist itself into a question mark of horror ... so real, scored itself in to his mind like a cauterizing iron ... he was not, since he hurried away, in time to witness the stranger several minutes later leaving the same establishment at a rhythm which was not usual among the clients who had sweated and relaxed for two hours ... more the pace of a criminal in a city full of police.

After Joseph K

Harry entered the stainless steel and chrome reinforced concrete gallery whose façade had been stressed against wood, hence a textured look. It was as is normal in galleries, white . . . and marble floored, with schemes of white arteries running through. To step in here was holy, it had the cool silent atmosphere of churches . . . the air was filtered through an electro-gauze mesh that singled out any impurities and regulated the temperature. The pictures were uncrowded and occupied space that was comfortable . . . In the centre of the room on what appeared to be an onyx dias and lit from above in a circle of blue light was a man kneeling and resting one hand (his right) behind him. In front of him, just obscured by some spectators, (H walked round) there was also a kneeling figure, crouched, of a woman with flaring red hair and cerulean blue dyed skin, vermillion nails and mouth. She was crouched over in an attitude of prayer and then Harry realised that the combination of the two bodies was deliberate and that the woman was in fact sucking the man's penis . . . her head movements were steady and unhurried and the man was equally undisturbed. The exhibition was partly devoted to conceptual art which had eluded Harry's interpretation but drew his curiosity. H wondered to what extent familiarity had inured the couple to celibrate

or enact this piece of conceptual art, and made
graven images in his skull of delights forbidden to
him in the freer air that they breathed. He tried not
to be aroused by the spectacle but take it casually as
the other spectators seemed to be doing . . . although
he did notice one silver-haired man smirking in a
knowing way as if totally unruffled . . . 'Oh we know
who you're fooling,' his bronzed winter tan seemed
to be saying and Harry smiled back at him . . . 'Yes, I
too get the jest,' but the man had missed
(intentionally?) the trajectory of Harry's smile which
flew off into space and then shrivelled not being fed,
and the tan let his own knowing smile fall onto a very
pretty young woman who had a hold of his arm in a
protective or proprietorial way which sent a filament
of sickness into Harry's craw at the thought of the
time that had passed since he last crooked his arm
for a woman. The two now looked at each other in a
way that spelt an infinity of secrets, disregarding the
naked couple, or perhaps, reminded so strongly of
their own closed doors that they became lost in a
reverie ... She looked too clever for Harry
anyway ... too knowing ... clever women he
couldn't abide, he preferred intuitive sluts or bright
Monroes. But intellectuals—Oh dear no! The posed
man and woman suddenly struck him as a parody of
Rodin's 'The Lovers' . . . the woman was resting now
and smiling quite gently as if the effort though not
tiring was never the less demanding, as a pose
essentially must be, and some of the audience smiled
back with her in empathy and not a little admiration,
as if she was proving something to all womankind,
some inalienable truth that her courage was
liberating for them. The man meanwhile had
redistributed his weight to the other arm but since he
didn't smile at the audience they didn't smile back at
him. Her cheek was resting against his knob . . . still

quite firm, 'amazing,' H thought, and she looked as if she might have been holding a carnation to her cheek ... obviously this can't go on all day ... could it? Perhaps they take a break for tea and return ... He looked for a title which rested on the plinth, one of those wooden triangles such as are used by bank tellers and it said simply ... 'The Circle Line Shall Survive' ... curious title and it left no association or reference that he could immediately discover to make the event any easier for him to understand. By now more people had filtered through past the doorman, looking resplendent in a navy serge uniform and gold buckle and glowing red cheeks such as seamen have who when retiring after long years at sea take jobs as porters ... but it's always their roseate glow that betrays their origins. Harry was tempted to test his little theory on the porter, anticipating the porter's chuffing guffaw of delight at the correct diagnosis, but the porter was far too busy searching people's bags since the provocative nature of the exhibition might tempt an unbalanced vandal or even worse. The girl had now resumed and lifted the man's rather sagging penis into her mouth which simply fell out lacking, after this interval, the impetus to keep it there ... the spongy tissue, glands and muscle had collapsed, no doubt caused by an exhausting day, naturally more so for the man, biologically, in sustaining concentration whereas the woman's effort was purely physical. As it dropped out a second time a couple of suppressed giggles came from the audience. One girl with cropped hair and prominent teeth had turned her back on the proceedings and had stuffed a handkerchief in her mouth to suppress a gale of laughter which otherwise might have exploded out of her. The gentle giggles nevertheless echoed around the gallery's vast spaces ... one man was concentrating very hard, he had long hair and dangling at his hips was a Nikon camera with a 200 ML lens and, the other appurtenances owned by serious photographers. H had once longed to study photography and possess a camera but somehow his career as a comedian, though not booming, made demands on his time ... even when not working, routines must be polished up, new gags learned and tried out, and his success such as it was, (he had worked for six out of forty weeks this year) was not royal but reasonable ... it kept him on his toes. He must be ready when the time comes and not be out of condition. That would be fatal. Sharp and ready, not for the pubs and the working men's clubs but the smart restaurants where they have silver service and the night clubs, music halls and even the theatres ... a friend of his once had two years in a West End run ... Two years! Continual employment ... H ran over the word, 'Two' as if he could savour the taste of it ... his agent realised his gifts ... that's good ... The male model by this time had recovered his aspiration sufficiently to hold it firmly in her mouth and the woman whose hair fell over the 'sight' in a great cascade, combed her finger through it, with a gesture of unveiling it from time to time, but it kept falling back in a waterfall of riot red ... blood red, he conjectured evenly. Now H was beginning to feel murmurs of appreciation within his groin ... he identified himself in the role ... could he do this, would he ever take even his trousers off in public, he winced visibly at the idea, a picture which occasionally manifested itself in the most acutely embarrassing dreams. He idly wondered if the man had already come or was planning it later or had not come and would not, so as to better preserve his act or exhibition ... He must really be tired but the definition of his triceps convinced H that his condition would enable him to sustain that position on his elbow for an unlimited time. H seldom went to galleries but this Sunday and for no particular reason he was tempted by the sound of an exhibition of European Conceptual Art and took the 172 bus, partly out of curiosity, partly to escape from the deadly boredom of a Sunday afternoon sitting in his gardenless flat where only his mother kept a watchful eye. On a sunny day, particularly on Sundays the claustrophobia of the flat would intensify and his ageing mother (he must get his own flat one day, just give me 20 consecutive weeks of work! . . .) would sit in a vague stupor reading *The Sunday Mirror* or *The Sunday People* and say 'Why don't you go out Harry, you're missing the sun . . . where's Micky, how come you don't see him no more? . . . or Betty?' . . . he hadn't seen this girl Betty for years but in the confusion of her sense of time the years somehow all merged into each other whenever she tried to recall an incident. He hated her suggestions which although well meant contained an implication of loneliness merely by implying that he had lots of friends . . . his brows creased and the skin on his scalp tightened . . . unpleasant flat, with his old room since childhood . . . he once moved out and was in demand in the small provincial towns for a quick likeable comic, whose jokes though not always up to date still had an innocent charm about them, derived from his awkward rendering of old favourites. He was attractive then, with curly hair and brown clear eyes . . . but his hair had thinned and his eyes had become a trifle bloodshot . . . the rending of his attributes left him no cover for an awkward delivery, which though once charming was now stale. Work lessened, and he moved back home temporarily, tried out new material in the kitchen using his father as a guinea pig. His dad always

laughed at his gags which relaxed H enough to really
be funny, since the essence of a good comic is not so
much his material but his delivery. But the audience
was not his dad and in the silence of the response
would tighten up and revive his old awkwardness.
During his brief return home his father died of
cancer which made moving out rather more difficult
until he had gained sufficient work to run two homes
. . . which he would do in time! 'Struggle maketh
man!' he propounded, loudly enough to be heard . . .
he fed himself these little homilies from time to time,
usually when under stress. The gallery was a
pecadillo of chance whim. He knew galleries to be
haunted by women, particularly foreign students
who would skim around armed with a note book . . .
He had two such affairs from his gallery sojourns
which were mercifully brief, since he held out no
interest for them after an initial sortie into his
personality, and neither they for him. All he wanted
was relief; one, as a receptacle for his semen and two
a crack at loneliness. He would have liked the affairs
to have lasted but saw no future for a foreign girl in
his life.One girl he did bring home to meet his
mother, and his mother had fallen asleep in front of
the electric fire with her legs apart and was snoring
loudly . . . Harry took the girl into his room where
they played some of Ravel's music and the golden
oldies selection on the gramaphone, and in spite of
his unwritten rule never to make it at home, was so
tempted. Whether this was through boredom or lust
or merely to do something that might render the
evening memorable in some way for both of them, he
could never be sure. As the fates would have it
mother wakes up *now* when she should be sleeping . . . she came in to say goodnight and was in time
to witness H's mauve protuberance steaming in and
out of the Dutch girl's embarrassed ass . . . a

spectacle surely full of horror for all three participants, and the outcome of the affair was to make the mother ashamed, Harry disgusted with his own flesh and resolve never to bring a woman home again. He had broken the sacred biblical injunction, 'do not uncover the nakedness of the son to his mother', even if unintentionally ... his mother (Oh no!) had had the sight of his monstrous lust, the thing most profane and secret in the strange relationship between mother and son, his erective potential, seen there glowing in all its rampant glory. Innocent mother, enter with flush and patchwork legs from electric fire to apologise for falling asleep exits with face as pale as dad's death mask. These thoughts cluttered and brayed in his skull as if to punish him for neglecting them, and whereby the invoking of them may in some way point to a moral lesson. He was then attracted to another exhibit, in fact only just noticed it tucked as it was in the corner of the gallery. It was of two people sitting at a table eating a chicken, which they picked at very gently and ate slowly since they must be there all day. There were less people surrounding this exhibit ... H almost preferred this one since he didn't wish to seem fascinated by lingering too long at the previous exhibit lest his motives appeared more base than aesthetic. The eating was fascinating and suprised H how interesting such a simple daily event could be ... I mean ... you do see it every day ... like at restaurants and at home with his mother ... 'would people queue to see me eat with her?' ... 'watch her put her teeth in folks, Oh! Now she's taking them out again.' The idea raised a dull pebble of laughter in his aching gut. The man and woman eating (male and female again, perhaps some link here) seemed very happy and would make appreciative gurgles and moans of delight and in between mouthfuls would say some words and then repeat the dialogue all over again . . . so obviously they were not making it up . . . How curious that by putting them on a plinth, they become an exhibit. Harry is an exhibit. He thought of the small stages in the Saturday night pubs with bad mikes that couldn't convey his jokes properly because of static, of the waxen droop of boredom that afflicted the customers like the plague . . . of his sickening loss of his sense of being . . . *even alive,* and why. Of his agent sitting watching him when there were only ten people in the house, and no one laughed, no one except one senile old lady who was unbalanced anyway and giggled for no reason and in all the wrong places as if afflicted by some private pantomime in her head, or perhaps the sight of a man standing on a small platform gently laved in grease which plopped on the floor and wearing the gibbering grin of an idiot was a subject for uncontrollable mirth. No doubt it was. Agent spat, 'audiences are shy to laugh when there are so few people in the house, you know that son.' The couple eating continued chatting . . . starting the loop again. He liked the way they spoke and were so utterly involved in each other's actions. Pouring out water for each other . . . 'pass the salt and pepper would you dear,' completely oblivious of anyone else around them . . . even if H was only two feet away they seemed totally unaware of his existence. He thought that if he touched them like you might touch a statue they wouldn't notice . . . would be completely impervious to him and he was tempted, was on the verge . . . 'Hell, they're in show business like me,' . . . could I be so oblivious, he thought . . . imperturbable, untouched in this white gleaming and antiseptic gallery . . . neon struck . . . could I get on stage and be that 'cold'. Yes, that's it. He hit his brain with the word as if assuming that this new knowledge that the event had imparted to him, could easily be transplanted onto him, and acted on that swiftly merely by the discovery of it ... 'an insight to heaven'. He still wanted to touch the hand of the woman that now rested casually on the table ... just to test his theory ... there he was, heart pounding as it never did before, as if to meet the challenge that would change once and for all the course of his life ... what could she do ... she couldn't kill him ... certainly wouldn't shout or scream. He stood in the middle of the universe of his thought, caught at a moment of a momentous decision ... his mother was at that very moment, unknown to him, weeping in her small, neglected and rather smelly flat ... weeping for him, for the son that she had hopes for, not for herself but for him . . . 'just some pleasure out of his life' and prayed every night for his success and a nice girl ... that they could live there for a short time until they found a flat ... they could even have her room. What did she need with a big bed now that the being who had made that amount of space necessary and had so amply and warmly filled it was gone out of her life forever ... the space even tormented her, filled as it was with the years of his soft breath on her back and his heavy arm over her shoulders ... so, she conjected, Harry and 'her', whoever that 'her' was going to be, would have the big bed in her room and, she would go into Harry's small room and his cramped single bed (he had the same one since a child) would more than fit her shrinking frame ... innocent old woman ... innocent that is of H's abhorrence of ever bringing anyone else there again ... and in her senility the incident had gratefully faded from her mind, while with Harry it had grown, even assuming monstrous proportions. He had, and dare he even admit the shadow of this to himself, wished, or, rather, would take some vestige of comfort in the tragedy of her death ... since she would take that image to the grave with her. So, as the world pursued its course around the sun heading for the extreme of its ellipse ... as the ice-caps were melting dangerously fast to the consternation of Arctic scientists, as the great St. Andreas fault was shifting and the Russians were completing their conquest of Mars with the first manned spacecraft to that planet ... Harry stood at the edge of time with the memories of his life engulfing him like a raging sea with each memory pulling him this way and that ... no rest or calm, so poor they were in joy. His mother prayed and that eased her tears, and made plans for a fictional woman ... his father we cannot here mention ... not now, except to say that he carried his portion of the world and did not pass it to others ... 'have I,' he thought, 'have I carried mine' ... and the pathetic gesture of wanting so badly to touch the exhibit's hand at this moment, and his heart beating for nothing ... *since he would do nothing* ... all this would have further reinforced his sense of futility had not a shriek wrenched him away and he was startled to see that the woman and man engaged in fellatio had been disturbed by an irate looking female in a hat who was wielding an umbrella and quite obviously had struck the naked woman's bottom with it since an ugly red weal had already begun to flower. H then turning to the other exhibit saw that they had stopped eating and were watching just like him ... they could be affected after all. On the way back home chewing over the days adventures on the 172 bus, H was suddenly struck by what the title 'The Circle Line Shall Survive' meant, for him anyway. He may have drawn a coarser meaning than one was meant to elicit but it obviously satisfied H since a smile broke from his face as the bus eased its way into Bethnal Green Road.

From My Point of View

'Of course I like the feeling of a full cunt,' she thought ' . . . I mean, who doesn't . . . and by full I mean choked full, stuffed full, filled with meat and do I question, whose meat? Yes, sometimes I can afford the luxury of discrimination and yes I do like to be kissed occasionally and not just wham, bam— put the kettle on love. I do like a man who's gentle and considerate . . . kisses me tenderly and doesn't just ram his hands up my skirt to his salvation, being a warm, wet, receptacle for his seminal deposits. Yet how often, sitting in my bed-sitting room do I get a call from someone I really like, and yet more often as not it's some Joe I met last year failing in his little black book (his fuck directory well thumbed) to find his usual bird clusters at home. Rings me— a vaguely remembered bird he met in an equally vague, party or pub . . . and what the hell . . . "let's try this one," thinks he . . . "Hallo, yes . . . who? . . . Joe who? . . . Oh!? . . . Well . . . OK, I'll meet you in the . . ." usually some grotty pub he hangs out in . . . not dinner, Oh no . . . "Thought we'd have a drink." He splurges out on two large gins in the hope of. Should say no really, hell rotten no! . . . But boredom mates uneasily with loneliness producing an offspring unbeloved, call desperation, fuck it . . . I brush my teeth to ameliorate my faggy throat, change my tights and knickers (or maybe just my knickers) fasten on my cap which I loathe wearing all the time and head out. Thus equipped to face the world at large with my little plastic membrane holding back the anxious creatures that the monster lets loose from his bow ... still, I'm out ... I'm in the air ... I'm using my voice and I see and smell ... I'm paid attention to. I am bought ... alright, so it's only a drink but I am bought it. I live like the rest of my human fraternity ... smile, do I and act like I too belong to the human race again, and not sitting on my bed wondering, as I stare at the walls of my prison sanctuary, wondering how I shall endure another bestial night ... tormented by the sounds of music being played in the upstairs rooms and their voices laughing Oh so loudly ... what can be so funny to make people laugh that loudly ... I never remember laughing like that ... what special ingredients fill their words and gestures to evoke such joy...perhaps it seems especially loud to me who am bathed in so much silence ... sometimes I can't sleep (so inconsiderate they) and their laughter always tinkles on into the small hours...but it's lovely when there is silence again ... then we are the same ... our silence is shared by all ... sitting there dreaming about kitchens with large wooden tables and chairs gathered round, cooking for my man's friends who come and chat idly, while I, pinafored, prepare...I like that ... liberation? ... I don't want liberating, I want imprisoning ... suffocating in the arms of my man) I want him to ask me to make special things ... I want him to *be* a bit late from the pub, what the hell, what's a half-hour or even an hour ... you enjoy yourself darling ... No I won't come to the pub I'd rather get the food ready and so I would, he's with me for life why hold back his separate precious hours, and I lay it out beautifully. My mother used to nag my father for tardiness of only ten minutes ...

lucky woman didn't know that to be alone and waiting for a man, any man, one might have to wait for years ... never mind ten minutes, she didn't know how lucky she was. Poor dad blustering in and chastised until his food wouldn't go down any more ... until the chastisement so consumed him that he vomited out a thrombosis brought about through a heavy surfeit of nag, and then ma *had* him, really and truly had him all to herself ... each day ... every minute was hers ... there he was upstairs, paralysed, in bed and whimpering for his cup of tea ... and wasn't she solicitous then, but of course who has to stay home and work to support us, why I am the inheritor of that raging twisting mouth ... or the deeds thereof since her venom's rewards fall to me ... and who wants a bride of 40 when eventually he kicked it, poor dad, and I left home ... hardly a virgin and barely anything ... except ... what could we do then, a girl of 20 and her boy-friend in the hall, standing up since sweet mum would hang around as if twisted for her own loss of male protuberance she therefore wished to share her empty hole with me or share her anguish ... "don't be too long dear," she'd whine from the living room ... "you've got work tomorrow," as if I didn't have work every day and face the gloomy and drab departments of perpetual boredom and obligation ... the poor guys in the cold hallway kissing me goodnight ... with a sharp frottage against my taffeta (it was then and when it spun around in the dance hall it lifted like petals surrounding a stamen) fed up guys rubbing their hard passion against me in the passage way, while mother is straining her ears from the living room ... and because it was a dark hallway and wretched ma calling, it made urgency for emission that more desperate, whereas a friendly cuddle on the couch and Billy Eckstein on the gramophone would have coaxed a more lasting appreciation ... The hall was furtive, made dark for speed not relaxation, as if what cannot be expressed in warmth and comfort but needs alleys and hallways, is something of a more dirty nature ... where the only demands are satisfaction ... so unknowingly but malevolently she condemned my young chances to dirt snatched and mangled ... wet pants and *no* love ... only their shuddering young bodies grabbing me ... their beards still soft ... their hips swivelling blindly against my mount of Venus ... and their poor throbbing hearts emptying their keen and youthful passion amidst sighs not unmixed with guilt for being condemned to alleyways, hallways and the dark recesses of tenements ... "Let's go up here love," he cajoles, at the inviting gloom of a staircase in some adjacent building smelling of cats and stale piss . . . "it's OK love, it's dark . . . please . . . it's alright ... no one can see us ... please ..." Oh ... their young kisses sweeter than wine ... but they seldom came back ... I yielded too easily ... too hurt by my strained home, I wished to compensate, for that uncharitable guilt ridden place by giving them that, which in their young impetuous hearts they hoped I'd hold on to ... their burning silken pricks were desperate as so often I'd let their juices run onto my hand but their hearts grew rigid as their members softened ... as if my hand in their eyes was scummed for ever. They wanted a picture of something else, a picture of something that should have been more precious to me. They liked coming ... gasping and quivering in the final sun-burst of their lust but wanted the ache to last and not be assuaged that easily ... too easily. They pictured too many other bodies being satisfied against this mound of flesh and lavender water (I used then and sometimes still do) ... and while the race was their's that night and peaceful dreams their's, the hopes of continuance died as if hope needs to be fed slowly for the thing one hopes for to have any real worth. "One must always struggle for something worthwhile in life," mother would simper ... but why should I make them struggle ... when I don't want them to. Perhaps I should force myself ... they seldom phoned again and the years drifted by with a succession of young hard bodies and yards and yards of their white stiffened skin bursting in my hands like a crushed fruit ... I became bolder ... Did I care? No! and for what ... the plague of parents, and of dad whom I truly did love, invests one at birth with such an awful magnitude of responsibility that one can't say no, and leave them to make do, can't leave home and make the nest I need to live ... breathe and play Billy Eckstein ... make coffee and gently dissuade their advances ... for now anyway ... win them gradually when trust grows from knowledge and affection and at least we could sit on the sofa and talk ... I'll cook beautiful dinners ... such whimpering idle romances drifted down like snow while some brute is fucking me under the staircase ... stockings torn, knickers around my knees and he's fumbling to get it in deeper but my knees are trapped by my knickers and won't spread ... he's cursing and pushing and hurting ... Oh so shameless am I now ... who cares now? ... what honour do I have to protect? ... No! I will not take my knickers off ... I insist ... shades of black comedy, I have my point of honour ... On my knickers I make the last stand of respectability ... my worn shreds of scruples ... let them fuck me but I won't go out of my way to take my knickers off and stuff them in my handbag ... "What am I, a whore?" ... he laughs and heaving me up by the ass he affords himself a good position and I feel his jets squandering themselves in

me and he withdrawing almost as fast . . . no passion
was extinguished quicker than this one. I stand . . .
weakly in that black staircase . . . my smells mingling
with the odour of dustbins and the vast effluvium
that humanity discharges into them . . . so much
keener are the smells now after the act . . . and watch
him wiping his prick with a soiled crumpled handkerchief. "You wanna borrow it love?" . . . his voice
held just the faintest note of compassion as if he too
unburdened of nature's blind demands—of no
matter how, and where, and to whom—empty it into
something!—was able to let float back into his heart
a slender recognition of a person with whom he had
shared an evening, from the first dance, all smiles
and jokes and carefulness to its ultimate shameful
ending.'

She went weekly to the same dance hall with the
twisting glass chandelier in the centre, and whereas a
few years ago was always accompanied by her friend
Doris—Doris having got engaged and then well and
truly pregnant, made it necessary for her to go
alone . . . All her friends got boy friends one by one
and although at first she wouldn't go alone and went
to the pictures instead, she found the dark wombs of
the cinema too unbearable and hated the end when
she'd walk home, made even lonelier by the romantic
and exciting lives of the screen heroes. One day she
decided to go by herself to the Mecca dance hall and
since Mecca is the holy and religious centre of the
world, the salvation for an entire race, it seemed
natural that she would find solace there . . . on
occasion she would bump into her friends with their
fellers and join them at their table, but always felt
slightly oppressed by their little knowing glances
which she'd exaggerate into hideous thoughts of
'what's the slag doing by herself' . . . and she would
gradually recline to the outer perimeter of the dance

floor ... in the shade so to speak and be dragged out to dance by one lonely man after another who first would eye her suspiciously and nervously. How a woman alone is a stigma ... and yet attractive ... dangerous, why alone? They think ... something in her casts her out from the norm ... the giggling girls ... the confident groups ... something that makes her slightly unwholesome, as if diseased ... yet offers up sweet, sickly goods if you want to take the risk ... still the element of danger ... makes her sought after by the kind of men whom the robust directness of youth would wilt ... who would not risk the light-hearted rebuff of young girls sure of their attractiveness who are waiting for strong, just as direct, young men ... but the lone figure in taffeta, now that is for me, man thinks, poses no threat ... only the remote element of a more nagging threat; no outward risk of humiliation ... possibly though the inward one, working on the vitals of the body or the brain ... She moaned inside herself ... 'how unnatural that I am a leper just because my mother had a raging mouth' ... the two things were somehow now inseparable, as if her mother had really cursed a twisted fate on her that she could not untangle ... so rather than try and change this situation she would make her mother eat her satisfaction. 'I like it here,' she mused ... Through the years she had watched the faces grow up from tender, young, energetic and pretty things to smart (still young), mascaraed ladies, teasing and jiving with their beaux and it gave her not the slightest taste of jealousy or remorse ... she was glad that she felt no bitterness but was able to enjoy the gaiety, even if the young and pretty things eyed her suspiciously as she, strange, caked make-up, wall-flower smelling too violently of lavender water, waited.

One night early in the spring there was a warm snap in the air ... it was the first time she could go out without the heavy top-coat and thus be spared the awful queue after the dance when she would have to stand with all the chattering excited girls giggling about who was taking them home and exchanging notes ... If she hadn't found anyone to take her home, she as often as not would persist right to the end of the evening when most people had been paired off. She would nervously await the remnants of mankind, the lonely and the plain, or the just plain psychotic who, also unlucky, would desperately eye the last possibilities and old tired wrecks to sort some salvage from the human female shapes that littered the outer ring. They, poor single women would feel even more vulnerable at this stage and creep nearer each other as if they too had friends, or ask each other for lights, pass nervous small smiles at each other, but still keep alert, since to pass out of the Mecca with a gentleman hooked to your arm was still something worth waiting for ... not to go alone and leave alone ... Show them—the young, the proud, the pretty—that I too can claim some happiness. So feeling spared of the queue and in the optimism that Spring brings, she was determined that night not to wait until the end and if nothing suitable came along, damn it—she'd go home. She went to the box-office clutching her money and set it down 'one please', but this time, and did she sense something as one man in an ill-fitting tuxedo leaned over the ear of the cashier, sense something like a cold blast? She did. For the lady in the box-office said ... 'I'm so sorry dear but I'm afraid you're barred' ... The queue of people behind her stopped their eager chattering, except for one joker, innocently unaware of the respect that one must pay in the face of tragedy, who sang 'Oh why are we waiting', to the

tune of 'Oh Come All Ye Faithful' .... 'So sorry,'
the lady repeated ... 'What have I done,' she thought,
'what have I done except act as a host to all those
multitudes, to ease their agony ... like a comfort
station you might say, *something you need when
you're desperate* ...' She stood there as if the
world had jolted to a halt and there could be no
place you could possibly go since one's home was
now a ruin of unmatchable stones ... she couldn't
speak ... stood there as if it hadn't happened as if the
cashier would witness the terrible effect which
needed no words and would be humbled by the
naked show of human agony and permit her to enter
what now indeed seemed like a Mecca. She didn't,
she just looked ... and eventually said, 'Would you
like to see the Manager?' but then as if annoyed by
the inordinate amount of time this trivial incident
was taking, the man in the box-office, who usually
doubled as a bouncer, nipped nimbly out and took
her to one side to let in the queue that had grown
considerably. They all glanced at her half curious,
half hostile ... what's the slut done now? scrawled
across their eyes ... the man in the tuxedo spoke
quietly, 'We don't want any trouble but you're
barred ducky ... alright ... know what I mean ...
nothing personal like' ... thought she, 'What did they
suspect me of? What did they suspect could be my
reasons over all these years for coming here ...
"Commerce" ... is that what's in their filthy
minds?' ... she said nothing ... she had become in
minutes flint from velvet ... He continued but
sensed a pain in her he hadn't expected ... especially
from a scrubber ... 'Give the place a bad name, on
the game you know ... get rid of it.' Higher orders
had thus embellished his mind with such commands
that he uncomfortably obeyed. 'You know,' he
added sympathetically, 'there's a club down the road

called "The Carousel", you'll be OK there.' He made
the suggestion based on the assumption that what he
had heard was true and therefore his advice was
charitable and not vicious. She knew the place it
was, and read only venom in his words and from that
instant began to hate the male part of the human
race. She walked away from the Mecca with its
twisting globe and ladies' invitation waltzes, with the
familiar sound that same band always had, from the
familiar smell and initial excitement when you first
enter that huge cavern wherein may lie your
future ... she walked away from it ... for ever ...
She stayed home for a year until poor dad, perhaps
willingly, seeing his treasured forty year old
daughter's plight, gave up the ghost in one almighty
shriek of joy.

She left home, determined to find that love-laced
sanctuary with a nice kitchen and sofa and saved for
a record player. For now, rents being high she lived
in a bed-sitter and found that loneliness just
suddenly doesn't disappear ... when you have lived
with it for so long it emanates from your entire
being ... when introduced even, you are afraid that
the stranger will sense it on you, as if some
disagreeable odour lingers that cannot be washed
out. Sometimes, though rarely, she was hauled away
when her local closed for an after drink party, more
to make up the number than any cognisance of her
being ... let alone her name ... but still she was
free ... 'aren't I,' she thought.
Perhaps the caller on the telephone this evening is
nice ... I remember speaking to someone who was
quite nice about a year ago at the office party ...
perhaps it's him ... she sprayed some lavender water
on her arms and not too carefully put lipstick on ...
'hell, what can a girl do at ten p.m. when she's been
sitting in drinking a few gins?' ... At a pub in

Kentish Town a guy named Harry was standing at the bar ... waiting.

Going Down

Coming up to surface with a mouthful of blood ...
cheeks reddened, with a thick gore glistening ...
looking for all the world like an impish schoolboy's
ravishing of a jar of strawberry jam, was not
Harold's idea of a perfect evening. Certainly he felt
no qualms in going down on her, since he truly
loved sucking ... it drew him that much closer to the
object of his need ... to knowing a woman with
shameless intimacy, to bring the inner sanctity of his
mouth to her groin ... how fussy one is, so particular
what one puts in one's mouth ... nose quivering at
yesterday's milk ... yet the heat of desire sacrificed
any cautious forethought in Harold's mind as he
sneaked like a moon probe across the white valleys
of his lover, whispering small licklacks over hills ...
nosing towards the musky heavy odour of Sybil's
cunt whereupon his head voyaging south to her feet
would stop, his forearm prising open her thighs ...
detecting the slight coppery or metalic taste which he
didn't find too pleasant, flanks spread apart like
opening a giant fleshy flower ... or she'd pour her
buttocks onto his hands whilst Harold's tongue
worked like an erratic snake ... up and down ...
pressing, chewing ... breathing through his mouth
as he licked and sensed her warm odours entering his
throat ... his cheeks were chafed sometimes, as if
she secreted some corrosive acid (could he have

59

licked up the residue of urine?) . . . did it matter down there dark, thigh strangled, hot, barely breathing . . . imagining in that florid hot-house the endless parade of his fantasies . . . moments in the underground, thick summer days . . . the sliding doors are open, a passing train in the other direction . . . its motion sends a little gust of wind into the carriage . . . invisible fingers delicately lift the thin cotton dresses, revealing all too briefly (rapid hands flutter, tug, cover) the gates of nirvana, Wallhalla, heavy in all colours, a riotous symphonic concerto of crutch . . . 'No, not one's earnest, coarse fingers in those greasy sockets *but* my mouth between those marble thighs' . . . such thoughts were the armoury of his endeavour, fuelling him to enable sucking Sybil's rather smelly cunt. He could be stoking the drain, blocked up in the garden, she stank so bad at times. So his habit of breathing through his mouth—more odourless that way—was safer . . . other times she smelt as fresh as new bread and earnestly swore how twice daily she'd wash her hole, even so . . . perhaps it was something she ate. She had soft pubic hairs, that was alright by Harold . . . he could no more suck the inside of a cunt whose garden had coarse (brillo-pad) hair, than lick assholes (reserved for beauties of extraordinary loveliness); shit and beauty in Harold's mind never co-existing, or at least as obviously as in a farty old slag . . . the thicker the hair, the stronger the smell, Harold fancied . . . even if not scientifically true, the feeling of it made it true so, sucking hairy mediterranean cunts, those hairy legged Greeks and Italians was *verboten* . . . he would retch at the idea, whilst black cunt though legendarily famed for magic properties was unimaginable horror . . . the downy hair of celts-saxons-nordics was fine and soft . . . Sybil was fair, reasonably attractive with good teeth and blue eyes—except the occasional rupture of acne on her back made Harold feel desolate ... sometimes in bed, he'd be alarmed to see the shining yellow beads of those eruptions and drive down fast, suck and forget ... would remember only the mouths about to speak, the impeccable panties, the frozen eyes, stern yet yielding as sirens, forbidding your mind to interpret the mystery of the picture the gentle wind exposed ... seeing these faces he could endure sucking at Sybil's greasy and sometimes smelly exit, while she would aid with her spit greased hand on his cock—her index finger one inch up his anus (concession in recent months) but sucking, god forbid— no ... she couldn't ... 'try—just once' ... 'OH NO I'D BE SICK!' 'Just a little lick then.' 'Please Harold, don't make me, give me time, I will when I'm used to you' ... so he gave her time ... for a year he had been travelling down to that brown cleft, opening to shades of pink ... and flaps and slivers opening like torn meat in the butchers, it was an animal, mysteriously armed with feelers or those monstrously swollen jelly fish floating in the Aegean ... sometimes he could take the daylight suck ... other times he could not bare to see it and took solace deep under the blankets and after he would surface looking like some insane deep sea diver, a mad drunk feasting on meths, or a predator fresh from the killing of some soft thing ... 'SORRY DARLING, OH MY GOD WASH YOUR FACE! I HAVE JUST COME ON. MY PERIOD! OH SHIT ... HAROLD I'M SORRY, WASH IT' ... Harold's face surfacing like a monstrous shark with bloody mouth disturbed Sybil since she didn't want Harold to see it ... 'stay there, I'll bring a flannel!' ... but Harold sensing something odd even down below ... more bitter than before, acrid even, that harsh taste ... he didn't stay, was already out of bed and even rushing to the bathroom aware of the red spore his fingers left on the wall as he hastily switched on the light ... 'Oh my God,' he spat as he spoke ... 'phphaaaaa!' Tried to wash out his throat under the tap *dare not* look, fuck no, look in the mirror! But on habit did and looked like he had been punched hard in the mouth ... calmly now he took the flannel and washed carefully every part of his mouth ... kept washing ... her words broke into the sound of the busy tap barely audible, scent of fear rising through them 'O.K. Harold? ... sorry love ...' So all these months he had performed his lingual duties to some indifferent smells and responses ... had even once smelled shit down there (what *had* she been up to) and the lady, too elegant to as much as put it in her mouth for five seconds without being ill ... menstruates in my holy mouth ... fucking menstruates ...

S. I'm regular . . . I don't understand.

H. Was it early . . . you think so . . . a few days?

S. It must have been . . . *(Diary hastily consulted)*. Oh dear I forgot the day! Don't look like that Harry.

H. You are a turd.

S. Harold I'm sorry . . . Harold? . . . No don't . . . don't, your mad!

H. *(clasps a large bread-knife while he shoves his cock in her face)*. Put it in your mouth . . . go on pig . . . **open**.

S. Yes Harry, but don't . . . please.

H. Just fucking open your mouth *(holds knife near her throat)* and hold my prick near the balls.

S. Yes Harry . . . harr . . . mmmn O.K.

H. Faster now you pig and squeeze my balls

at the same time.

S. *(choking).* mmmmm! . . . chchch! . . .
NOOOO! *(withdraws mouth).*

H. I'll kill you Sybil, so help me . . . SUCK
IT!

S. O.O.O. Harry . . . don . . . mmmmn . . .

She hadn't a bad mouth and once she started seemed
to go at it with an eagerness which wasn't purely the
result of Harry with his pink scrubbed face kneeling
over her with a bread knife. But bore more the effect
of one, who in having no choice decides the lesser of
the two evils was to go ahead and enjoy it. He
came... screaming... and she didn't flinch but
licked every drop down ... licked it clean ... was it
retribution for her accident, or was there something
indefinable and unspoken in her which begged the
threat of supreme violence in order to unlock what
she desperately wanted to give (dare not admit her
tastes) longed always to have taken ... as she lay
calmly beside his sleeping body ... his face broken
by waves of peace she felt no more fear and even
thought with gratification of her curse... his poor
bloody mouth... she could not restrain a thin smile
escaping from the corner of her lips... naturally
Harold didn't see it.

The Secret of Capitalism

I have a room...that is most important...I have a room in an old house but the house is mine. So I have tenants...so far so good. I have a nationality and speech. All the things that bring me together as one being are in and outside me. I have a house and a woman in the house...that's as it should be...I mean, a man should have a woman and have a house to deposit her in so as to be adjacent to him and vice-versa. She also has a room and visits his room—so she has autonomy which is also most important. They can look out of separate windows onto the streets—which brings me to my street—so I have an address and I receive letters. Without an address nobody will write you a letter...so an address increases the possibility of written communication, also a postman will visit you and occasionally ask you to sign a book for special letters. Your house is recorded in the Town Hall and is part of history, which you as occupier will help to make...the house will always be there, perhaps for ever. It is in the Deeds of the house and recorded in ancient maps and scrolls and charted for sewage and water flow. All the mysteries of the tides that come to and flow away from the house are now yours. So, I have a woman, a house, nationality, lodgers, own room, language and postal possibilities. Also I have inside and outside two cats . . . both are tortoise-shell but

65

they are not related . . . one of the cats has one ear which lends her a distinctive air, and both of these cats play in the garden—which is also mine . . . so now you may see how a human being is put together gradually to form a composite entity. Having a house you will also possess everything within the house and necessary to the house's comfort but since these things can be bought as effects they are not worth mentioning except insofar as they may throw some light on you. So far nothing here is mentioned except the house that is actually bought since you cannot buy the street or the postman or letters from a friend, or a woman . . . not in this particular case . . . so these things are of a more related nature by the act of getting a house . . . in the house and to possess it I have a mortgage which is an ancient document, not my mortgage but mortgages as such date back in origin over a thousand years. I have also a bank in which I deposit or withdraw money . . . therefore like the rest of this society I have a Bank Manager. I have an agent for work as an actor but for some reason they never get me any work, so I have a bad agent. Also I have an administrator and part-time secretary who has an office on the top floor of an old building which is seedy although her office is a model of order . . . she has an inside toilet which she needs a key to unlock and then locks up again, although there is nothing to steal except turds. I have an Accountant, a Lawyer and a Dentist plus an Arts Council Bursary. I have plays, stories and many photographs . . . the photographs are of a holiday in Greece and one old one of my sister and myself in Brighton sitting on the wall of the Black-Rock Swimming Pool, I was 10 years old at the time. I have a Literary Agent (I forgot to mention her) . . . yes, she is a woman and she too has a secretary and so indirectly they are put to my use, therefore you could say that I have 2 secretaries, a further one who also works part-time for me, even a small part of the time and everything or anything that influences her: i.e. her mother feeding her, her boy friend kissing her or abusing her too: all this serves to affect the five minutes or so every day that she devotes to me in answering the phone or writing letters on my behalf. So, her boy friend and her mother and father all serve me in some infinitely small but ineluctable part of the complex tapestry which is my life. And who do I serve? I serve all of them to a degree in that I provide them with a marginal sense of purpose. I serve whom I work with and I serve the audience but they in effect also serve me and partially belong to me... since it takes a hundred or more to serve me at one sitting but it takes only one of me to serve them but to serve them I am helped by able-bodied people who also serve me as I serve them. The mute point of who serves who depends on a particular form of philosophic thought which may be elliptical. It also depends on who thinks it first. If the person who is serving me thinks that he is being served by me, before I can state that I am being served by him, then psychologically he may be at an advantage, purely in the thinking of it... first. Sometimes 200 people will come to see me in a play or see my play... to reach the theatre they will occupy 200 spaces in buses, cars and taxis and this puts out another 200 who were wanting those particular services and so on with ever-diminishing effects... So, one can say that the 200 have washed, eaten, planned, telephoned each other and affected throughout this activity a further 1000 people (switchboards, restaurants, cars, parking space attendants), communicated, read newspaper reports, met each other and eventually walked up the stairs of the building, were anticipatory, sat down and watched the play. At the end of the play, 200 people got up and left the building and in their consequent actions disturbed or affected another 1000 people. In slightly poetic terms they resembled a small tide of humanity seeping into a particular crevice in the rocks and then being pulled out again to dissolve into and swell the greater mass, making no impression on the mass and yet essential to it. The rocks are again revealed much like the seats in the theatre when everyone has gone, except that the inflowing tide has washed clean the rocks whereas in the theatre a char lady goes round in the morning cleaning up. The only cleansing effect might be the purging of unclean spirits and the dissolving of agony through identification. These are side effects and bear no relation to the greater theme of possession. These people go home carrying within them the germ of my play as by contamination and the words and actions of the production flit around inside their minds which may last for days or even for years, and may even effect the way they move or think about certain subjects . . . consequently these people may be serving you indefinitely if not consciously. Of the 200 who come each night, some will die this year and others next year. Since there are approximately 1000 per week in a good week, it would be true to say that some may be dying during the play. The condition of the audience will vary, unrelated by what they are seeing since they brought their own mood with them from sadness to a state of pleasure, others will be in a state of jealousy and others will be made envious by what they imagine is a nice way to earn a living since they are relieved of the boring drudgery of putting a play together and dealing with the temperament of actresses. Some women in the audience will be in the time of their period and wearing appropriate safeguards ... when they talk afterwards in the bar, loudly and pontifically, an X-ray through them would reveal tights, corsets, Tampax, soiled underwear. If one could see through their clothes they would not seem so affected, in fact they would appear silly. Animals never appear silly since they do not wear Tampax or tights. And how ridiculous a dog would look with a cigarette sticking out of his mouth. And yet a human looks more ridiculous. But humans are convinced they look alright because everyone looks stupid in one way or another. During the week the 200 people will talk to another 1000 people, assuming that they mention it to at least 5 people each during that week which is quite likely. So 1200 people will be affected each performance in a greater or larger degree, like a tiny drop of water receding over a limpet as the tide claims it back. So during the entire week, 7200 people including taxi drivers and the milliard diverging pressures will be brought to a streaming confluence by one person moving with a steady pace to his goal. I will be in part responsible for this effect by being a small pool or crevice which will trap a certain part of humanity. They will serve me by washing over me and (metaphorically) leaving behind some of their treasure for the experience. If they pay a pound they will have contributed, if middle class, one hour, after taxes have been paid, of their labour. So they have contributed not only one and a half hours of concentration plus one hour to travel to the theatre and buy their tickets, but at least another hour in labour, and it will take them after they have retrieved their coats, another hour to go home and so all told one has a gain of 4½ hours from each person. That's if one could find a way to use those hours. Of the 200 in the audience each night, 130 would have had a bowel motion that day and 15 would have had sexual intercourse; 2 would have had sex before coming to the theatre and approximately 17 will have sex after... indirectly affected by what they have seen... I will, in a sense, be in the way of their sex, I will affect the quality of their movements, especially if they were soothed or gratified by what they saw or sensuously aroused. I may therefore increase their satisfaction or curb it. They will talk at length about the play, or briefly. On the other hand they may quarrel violently with each other as to the meaning of the piece since it is open to interpretation and, through this conflict, the man will see he has nothing in common with the woman and decide that night to leave her since this particular play stimulated them both to a statement of intent and measure of their own observations and sensitivity. On the other hand he may, if inflamed, decide to kill her since this is the last straw and he is aghast at how stupid she is and is excited by an overcharge of adrenalin. If he does this I will have a murder on my conscience to a slight degree, diminishing in return to the extent of his own psychosis. This audience comes from separate parts of London and the world and are all brought together by a common interest to one particular building. They will share an experience as one mass no longer part of an anonymous tide but a related one. They will laugh at appropriate lines and hear and smell each other. At the end they will put their hands together in appreciation and this same mass of people will never ever meet again although they were a party to a particular experience and brought together by chance. They will never exploit this strange fact. You may think that the same thing applies to someone on a bus and that the group of people on that particular bus were congregated together by the same laws of chance and likewise could exploit that. However, that is not quite a fair analogy since to choose that particular play suggests a wealth of under-currents, taste and inclinations, curiosity and desire particular to the 200 who chose to see that play out of 10 million people. The critics come on the first night and write about you. Their reviews are read carefully or glanced at, picked through, raced through, mostly ignored, read anxiously, audaciously, arrogantly, sadly or happily, even cynically by 1 million people in 5 or 6 papers. 3 million times will your name be printed in offset litho and the next day someone else's new play will crush your name and work into limbo but not quite...for a few moments that day you shake hands with the King; for those few seconds that you are there under his gaze (he representing the nation) you hold history in your hand, the last line of 1000 years of kings...and so you hold onto that moment. If one froze that moment you would be there for ever, and time having a subtle way of stopping now and again gives that impression. How does that audience know that it will ever leave the theatre. As far as they are concerned, they are there for ever. It is only in their knowledge that it must end. But one can never be really sure, especially since one is deprived of certain sensory measuring stimuli such as daylight deepening into night or changes of temperature. In the theatre there is no time that can be measured since one is bathed in a constant light and the steady drone of words and sounds may never end, but it does and in that way lies sanity: only in the sure knowledge that it will. In the same way the critic's columns focus the nation's attention on you 3 or 4 million times over and if a certain paper reviewed it, no matter what copy of it you picked up it will be there, it will not subtly change...but later, for instance the following morning, people in the poorer areas are wiping their asses and wrapping their chips in your hopes for immortality. Others are throwing it on the litter heap of yesteryear's editions where the corpses of old news welcome you on the heap waiting to be used for other purposes. You may find yourself in toilets that one sees in parks and public places. The newspapers are torn up into squares... and on one of the squares there you are, or one-millionth of you is finding yourself wiping clean the excessive excrement on some stranger's ass. But, as she or he craps, they may have taken into their hands the strips of paper in readiness but, in glancing down with the idle curiosity that people have in toilets examine a bit of news before reaching their final apotheosis and then glueing your legend to their sphincter. As they read it, during which time they have laid well tunnelled and twisted lavas of molten shit, they are seized by a sudden notion (time and place being conducive to deep thinking) to see this particular play. 'Hmmmmmm'... they murmur... 'How interesting'... Crappppppbbrasperyyy-thpp...! This is possible... but to get back to other things besides the critics who serve me with their reviews... I do have other things; for instance, I have ulcers. I have to drink milk when they start inflaming me, when a little worrisome fire is ignited in my belly in the upper part... I have a fridge for the milk in which I also keep the cat food. I can still remember when we didn't have fridges years ago in the suburbs and had instead a cupboard with mesh netting... this is about the time when I had that photo taken with my sister in Brighton. Everything went off quite quickly and the milk was kept under running water in the basin to keep cool. I have had my fridge for 8 years and my mother gave it to me, who had it for ten years before that... so it is a sturdy fridge, you might say. I do have a friend or two ... probably two reasonably good friends and several acquaintances and two lots of neighbours ... my friends, if I could count up all the people that I know reasonably though not well, would be about 50 ... and perhaps 10 of those intimately, if not lovingly. Each of these 50 whom I know reasonably well, perhaps know another 50 people reasonably, so I will have a possible cache of 2500 people who may be aware of me reasonably, and these 2500 may know another 50 which would bring me only twice removed the possibility of knowing or the knowledge of 125,000 people, which is a lot ... so, surrounded by my house, my fridge, room, woman, spare room, windows, Literary Agent, photographs and, oh yes, I forgot my books. These 200 books bring to me the accumulated knowledge of 200 people who acquired this knowledge throughout their lives and the experience of other books plus teachers and families of, say, 100 per writer, which brings me the distilled experience of 20,000 people all together ... all in my one room. The million who have read me in the columns (I now begin stocktaking), the thousands who have seen me on the stage and the dozens for whom I have unconsciously affected their sexual experience, my two cats, my Accountant, Lawyer, part-time secretary, two neighbours and a garden, my ulcers and the memories of an old cupboard, a street which is part of history and an address, the possible knowledge of 125,000 people which is a lot and the possibility of stopping time. Plus the woman upstairs ... surrounded as I say by these points of reference which eventually must run into millions ... I wonder why I am often sad, lonely and desolate.

Pictures

At approximately 10 strokes a second, he calculated, 600 to a minute and aided by olive oil, Brylcreem or vegetable oil—the best lubricator but with a tendency to the finest insulation—at 600 strokes a minute, three minutes would produce 1800 strokes, then there would be the thankful emission from his grateful prick... his eyes fixed at the usual spot on the ceiling and made a tight link to that crack or hair which seemed to be painted in (loose hair from decorator's brush?) and across this link, like an electric beam, travelled a lexicon of images, so inventive was the mind at this state, the translation of this source of inspiration to a painter's hand would have filled the National Gallery... a thousand variations of Judith's thighs, the spread open red mouth of her womb flashed on and off the ceiling like a crazy strobescope, the pictures twisted and dissolved into swollen vulva's, deep dark shadows opening up to snow, glistening misty forests and tropical dank flowers unpeeling... the cock strained at this point to brace itself, a snake about to spit, but flagged again from over-exposure, these particular movies had seen too many re-releases... new scenes flashed on dredged up from the ancient vaults of his mind, some would tend to get confused like an actor in repertoire mixing up his parts, or he'd jump-cut from scene to scene (incredible editor) hold one for a few seconds longer, or freeze a frame, slow dissolve, leap from mouth to mouth and cunt to cock in three or two shots, old fading experiences mixed with fiction... hot greedy mouths, men's, from infantile experiences, and pubescent painful experiences which changed into unsuccessful affairs, then fictionalised into brilliant seductions; lone female fingers prised out his cock and lovingly swallowed it... but the images based on fiction did not have the staying power that truth etched into the mind, and faded only too quickly leaving that same crack of hair on the ceiling... and the silence ... broken only by the soft susurus; the whipping flesh and quickening breath, and the lone solo instrumentalist in the room, empty usually, except for a prostrate outstretched body tapping out the relentless morse-code on his cock... does any one pick up the signals? Lonely, dedicated wanker of the endless nights, surrounded by the riotous horny guests of his imagination... again the men's mouths; experience of darkened cinemas, cheap flea-pits in the remote suburbs, running *Spring in Park Lane* to the memory of humiliation and fear of getting caught, furtive eyes, sticky handkerchiefs, smelly Turkish Baths; these had, between moments of electric stimulation also a vaguely deadening effect. The whore who watched him spill his seed into her discarded knickers was good... he was primed to come on that but no, it would leave him with a bad memory at the end ... so he switched it off and flashed Judith back on (her greasy black knickers held the stage for a further 200/300 strokes) and then he projected a whole series of flashbacks with the speed of a remote-control slide projector... swelling vast cock exposed to the hungry eyes of Scottish teacher (incredible grip she had), emptying vast quantities of spunk into the endless open mouths of women like the beaks of hungry birds...on and on, fiction smearing onto fact, male converging into female...the cock, proud strutting creature, was tiring of the years of service of penal solitude within the shackles of this man's fist, wearying of the endless roles...was it this man's joy, his solitary guard against the vivid constraint of truth, the EMPTINESS, MUST IT BE A WALL OF FLESH AROUND IT AND HOW LONG CAN IT BE SO, THE WEARYING FLESH?... Soon it will be over ...but to end on a good one...it was straining to spurt...to send the owner back to the limbo from whence he came, and the flesh back to the comparative sanctuary of darkness and peace...the rhythm slows down...not so fast, hold it back...wh*oa* boy not so fast! Hold it back... do not spill the precious lotion in vain on the memory of some old slut...hold fast the gates until the cunt computer makes the right selection for a hit...a whisper 'more oil'...the needle of his desire scanning back and forth every possible combination of pictures...yes...the girl in the tube...her crossing legs accidentally exposing to his snaking eyes the instant explosion of her triangle (moon-white—sanctified by Diana white), she repeated this action which made him squirm for the rest of the journey, hands in his pockets he mutilated his flesh and during this time she did not refuse him the sight that was his altar on that voyage through the black tunnels of the city . . . she left the train delicately, uncrossed her thighs more overtly; do you see the contours, her thighs soft white tender dreamy... she's gone...the ensuing adventure of what might have happened had he had the courage to follow made many an interesting story and often provided the perfect climax to his jerkings...he would start at the same point and go over it carefully, second by second . . . the colour of hair, smile, the shape of leg, shade of underwear . . . it was beautiful; just once or twice before reaching his conclusion he'd interject with Judith to test the strength of his present story, and satisfied that Judith was endowing the performance with far less fuel, continued the fantasy in the train, the smile . . . the legs . . . faster, the colour of knickers . . . faster . . . mix now with spit (mortar and pestle) up to normal speed . . . 600 a minute, even faster 700 . . . 750 . . . the picture on the ceiling increasing to intensity . . . her open joints, his fingers .engaged in thick warm flesh discovering the new continent . . . her panties were a holy veil across his face . . . HIS cock became quite still, breathless, waiting for the explosion. The INEVITABILITY OF IT . . . HIS flesh was blushing like a throttled colonel, (he was in love with her desperately) . . . a thick pearl formed in the smile of his knob like a tear . . . (desperately loved) (POURING) he licked . . . (SPURTING IN TWO RISING JETS) . . . her . . . pumping out the last spasm in a thin web still reaching high . . . smelled her, (first strangling the last juices of his cock's throat) . . . loved her always . . . the picture faded abruptly . . . leaving the crack with the hair . . . he wiped the cooling spunk off his belly with four or five sheets of Kleenex . . . you could depend on the girl in the train.

She or a Day in Brighton

As she ran for the bus her hair would jump and
impersonate a waterfall spilling over a cataract. The
sun almost heaved itself out of the sky this morning
like a difficult birth... it poured from torn wounds
yellow tears into the sea. Suddenly, before the
contraction of a pupil exposed to sun from woolly
cloud, the sea transformed itself into a lake of
emeralds and then a cold palace of verdigris...
marmoreal... then purpureal. White flecks are spat
up as invisible demons blow down... white flecks as
the blue paint which is chipped away, exposes the
underneath... from the sea Clytemnestra gathers
squids whose special ink dyes the silks that
Agamemnon will tread on his triumphant return
from Troy . . . she will plunge her dagger into
the same silk, wrapping him in it as he steps from his
bath... The sea smells sharp today, tangy, fishy,
ozone laced... its smells filter through the curtains
and linger on the walls, its invisible antennae crawl
through the bricks and under the window panes...
slide across her pillow over several thousand fine
golden spears that sprout from her skull... they lie
like a field of corn... golden and still... so her hair
lay like flax ready to be woven... and the smell of
the sea crawled over the pillow and into her head, up
her nostrils and floats over the special nerve colonies
of her brain begging for recognition... and the

gentle susurus as claws of wet green tickled small shingle, tinkling, whispering, found the curvature of her ear, spinning round the tunnels of flesh and beating tiny taps or small filibrations on her drums...the two effects (smell and sound) were conjoined as if by plot...those waves would also serve to prise open the memories that will seep out gradually and hover in the Sunday morning breakfast air smelling of tea, bacon, toast, polish and dead things...like the memory of old loves and loving, perpetuated after the corpse of a kipper has been devoured and is fleshily stimulating the devourer...the tray is left quietly outside the door . . . the tea and marmalade make a small fire glowing inside the packages of skin that swell and yield...those presents to one's partner in the early morning blue with white buttery tinged clouds peering through the window...her Edwardian nightie lay on the bed like a promise of eventual fulfilment...after we arose it was lain across the bed by the chambermaid as though a live thing was still in it...it was silk and the touch of it gave pleasure to the maid who would hold it in both hands and on opening them, let the nightie pour from her hands like it was a living thing...like a cat was pouring out of her hands.

Stardom

The gases in the universe are floating and spinning away at the speed of light, away from us, everything expands. The spirals of millions of stars is an emission from the collision of invisible gases gripping, passing through each other, exploding a chain of circumstances that will be repeated microcosmically. Carbon and Helium fuse and send twisting away from itself, rolling over and over, one thousand million stars. In one man's emission from a full penis will be a thousand million spermatozoa, ... these sperms took forty five days to reach maturity . . . out of all of them only one valiant strong tailed beast will survive, only one will in its travels along those dark river beds of blood and orgasmic secretions find a world to penetrate, from a journey through the warm labyrinths of inner space the equivalent of millions of miles. Blindly its will, such as it must have, and desire to be, guides it to penetrate the celestial orb which comes floating down to meet it, they greet with little formality and lock in an embrace that will not cease. Not until anyway one has wrested the secret from the other. Thus an emission of sperm resembles a galaxy, in a silken glittering silvery web of froth; floating in space, it would spiral like the milky way or like cream in coffee, or paint in oil, or ink dropped into water...The gases create the emission by confrontation and osmosis, some mad god is populating the universe with the wild excesses of his passion, if there are ten thousand million stars in our galaxy the Milky Way, our own village, and one thousand Milky Ways, soon where will we find room to move? will not space be obliterated through overpopulation? However the interstellar gallactic social heads will control space over-pack by a series of thermonuclear suns that will go spinning into new orbits obliterating as they go. Errant asteroids will be armed and sent on new paths pulled out of their normal gravitational orbits and collide with living world centres.

At that particular time I may be just at the point of spraying my burning vaporous seed into the womb of an earthly flesh garden to grow more cherubic plants of plasma/bone/thought, when the end will happen, my own universe be disintegrated and plans of future galaxies destroyed at source. My body, stained with all her viscous stigmata, my emptying vessels screeching from hot pipes, the creatures spitting, racing, hurtling through the black hole (a giant succuum, or sucking vacuum), my teeth breaking themselves on raw bone in the absurd excesses of passion and my fingers brilliantly ringed in tunnels of flesh-warm. At that moment, the moment when my spine receives the benediction of a fugue played by her delicate fluttering fingers, will she, dark, tight pupils accept the vision through the window of a giant sun scorching through the night like a vast lion about to devour us? Fires already raging everywhere and still one million miles away, travelling at 2/16th of the speed of light, the decision will have to be swiftly made of how we wish to spend our last five earthly minutes or climb into the time-machine and hurtle off to a more clement century.

Eventually we were too deeply locked into each

other's system to disentangle, without subsequent emotional damage, she held fast to my hips until she came...screaming, and I too followed, and just then the fire was upon us and sucked the air out of our lungs before crushing the planet into a charred heap leaving a black hole ... We were just in time.

The Assless Dictator or Homage to Miss Gascoigne

The sea joined sky, married—flowed into each other, mixed—fertilised new colours—became an inseparable sheet—of slate, jade, and deliquescent marble veined with cracks and splits of white...the mists move over the water ... glazing and caressing, rolling over the waves, will roll over the clawed creatures scuttling...August 4th is a day of peace ... I sit outside the hotel in a wicker chair ... the receptionist wears a thin, fine Victorian blouse over a gossamer thin bra or halter that can only weigh an ounce...her breasts are heavy but not too much, more a gentle heaviness...almost plangent, soft weight, warm crushables, squeezable, sway very delicately...the nipples dark, just barely perceived by the scanning eye that crawls over the body like a green leech ... the sea now divides itself from the sky as if it had dripped out of heaven and now floats heavily...the division while clear is not yet sharp but a soft bleeding in of colours...the edge of blotting paper...the sea is heavy and the small waves curl over each other like small kittens rolling and playing and showing flecks of white paws...the atmosphere smells clean and fishy, sea-weed salt and spray, but is cool and damp, and while the sun beats down heavily and invisibly the clouds spread out to prevent us having any of it ... yet thin small tracks of yellow almost seem to seep through but become scattered...soft bodied sea anemonies flop and squirm in the glaucous green for them, for smears of sudden warmth. In her pants rests an immutable secret, subject to the same forces as the sea...her underskin softly holds an active small beast...this beast has a maw which gently holds your future and your present might...and is the entrance into an embryonic cave as surely as is the sea...the sea spills out life from its crucible fertilised by the sun's shafts that break themselves into the green...the sea wears away at the cliffs...the cliffs, friable and stiff, crumble over the years...they crumble like a giant edifice topples in slow motion, it crumbles and is sucked into the sea whose thin rasping claws gather it up...small shelled creatures make homes there and dart in and out with delicate antennae the colour of coral...her caves tempt you crazily to hold discourse with her eyes...the first orbits of the journey to unknown spaces in her vast and fertile universe of untold delights . . . her eyes are brown and moving, within which galaxies, harbouring many different systems, can be seen evolving...the sea's horizon remains in her eyes . . . the tides float across them...when the tide comes in I will enter and be carried in her body's liquids to her inner depths...I will thrash and beat inside her and she will take and give...enough for me to dissolve and crumble into her . . . which I do willingly, painfully and lovingly...she watches this event with a steady familiarity borne by untold millions of years genetically locked in some clue of memory...her eyes are full of this happening...she lazily watches the emptying of my eyes while far below and deep within her...fathoms deep...small forces are meeting the invaders...they will know what to do...they will harvest them...but only one will get through...he will give a message upon which is inscribed and in code, the secret of the universe.

Gross Intrusion

'Gross Intrusion' is the term given by auto-engineers when a car penetrates another causing death or injury to the occupant of the weaker car, whose body structure may have caved in too easily due to lack of what is called 'Structural Integrity'.

The guy poured some olive oil out of a bottle on to the palm of his hand, set the bottle down with his free hand and rubbed the olive oil first into both palms then onto his prick...then he casually, and not before checking the nail of his index finger plunged the same finger into H's ass... took his finger out again as if satisfied with its location and pushed his prick in which entered slowly and gradually as the shocked sphincter was having to adjust its role from delivering to receiving. Slowly yielded the flesh and its co-ordinated network of fine muscles... they relaxed between moments of revulsion when all the sphincter wanted to do was to purge itself of the monster that was threatening it (what kind of turd is this?) and harness its forces to an almighty gesture of expulsion when the hole would resemble the iris of a camera at its smallest aperture, but each time the sphincter relaxed itself for a further intake of power that might crush the invader the cunning prick would advance further into his fleshy ranks. It was painful now as it made its inexorable journey against the natural grain of his tunnel... it pushed, quelling any resistance, and each advance into his groin was followed by an almost involuntary withdrawal affording the active guy ecstasy since longitudinal rubbing and latitudinal squeezing is what petrassage is all about... the push in needs to be followed almost immediately by a slow coursing out, as if having prepared the way by its initial attack the prick too withdraws to rally its forces to return and joyfully confirm its victory, and so as not to lose ground the next movement in was even stronger in its thrusting power. For H, pain as it went in, and the incredible sensation as the prick withdrew, of shitting, plus the fear that he actually was and half expected a strong smell of shit to come floating up to his nostrils. H was not familiar with these sensations which are part of the ecstasy of the passive recipient; that sense of possessing a cunt in one's ass, a strong centre of feeling whose payoff on being buggered is a sensation of shitting (the two, somehow, ineluctably combined). H was not yet refined in this more arcane pleasure of lovemaking, and to this end his curiosity became a seductive devil that tempted him to the present experiment. But this curiosity was born less out of the passion of the explorer than out of an evil growth that fed itself in the dank fields of waste and boredom and the desire to flagellate his skin and spirit into some sense of being alive... and needed. This sense to be needed had perverted itself as it twisted away from its original course through lack of fulfilment, and careered blindly to another world... any world where he could be of use. Or used. In normal times he would distribute his golden load one way only, disturbing and caressing a whole battery of nerves that clicked on, as the sphincter, like a chief electric nodule sensatised the area; and the charting of a torpedo-like turd to the lower depths was subtly and satisfyingly felt, right to its last tapering tail which reluctantly leaves, vacating the area that stretched and contracted for its expulsion, and as soon as it hit water the great lower intestine or ass-hole was already mourning its loss. Its loss of nag in the bum by the tenant that satisfies too. The ass was a normally dormant theatre compared to the sheer activity of the crazy twitchings in the tubes of flesh hanging and lolling in the front. But certain and gradual reversals were taking place... the desire dormant for so long was beginning to stir as if awaking from a long sleep. H would vaguely try to cast it back to oblivion but it had incubated for too long and wanted out. Who or what planted the seed one cannot here go into . . . suffice to say that it existed. H remembered those heaving and hot summer shits in the fields feeling the motions of almost burningly large turds coursing out of his system in the shape of men's pricks, so huge at times, even the size of pricks. Did that one come out of my tight little rosebud? H would simper to himself, occasionally delighting his skull's porn-box by gently inserting his little finger up his ass and feeling with wonder at how tightly even his little finger would be gripped, and thrillingly and frighteningly would conjecture how on earth the hard, large cocks of men would or could penetrate him. So, he would sit in the fields distantly gazing at the horizon with misty and soft-focused eyes, dim for pleasure... the pleasure of feeling so much in his hole. This new or gradually awaking discovery of an unexplored planet of delights within his being led him to fantasize about being taken unaware as he sat there with naked loins, by an irate farm labourer and his mate who would be so incensed at the sight of H's naked joints that they would rudely throw him to the ground and slide their pricks up his still moist ass. In these moments H felt indeed like a quivering virgin. Now was reality... now was the pain... the guy was holding on to his prey like a terrier holds a rat, pushing deeper and deeper... so deep it must be wounding me, H thought... but he mustn't complain or shout out... that would seem so silly. The man supported H under his belly pulling him up to encourage him onto his knees and almost making H impale himself on the stranger's weapon... odd words came out from the man between quick hard breaths... *'Hurt? You O.K.... Enjoying yourself cocksucker?... Wan' it deeper?... I'll fuck your head off!'* . . . as passion grew inflamed, the stranger's text became more ribald and even ridiculous... *'I'll kill you when I come you mother-fucker!... I'll eat you up you bastard!'*... mixed with a reasonable variety of *'Ooohs'* and *'Heyssss'* and *'Haaaaaas'*... *'Honey Oh honey you make me feel so good!!!'*... H said nothing but allowed it all, or rather submitted to it... feelings now spent if they were ever there to spend... sex sucked out of his being the way a raging fire sucks the oxygen out of a room... as if sex had never existed except in his mind... or in the fields with his little finger probing the little mouse of sensuality that had errantly taken lodging there... or in the swollen bulges of men, in their nude swarthy flesh stiffening in the illicit camouflaging steam of turkish baths; the haven of all the third sex. Now it was pain . . . and yes, even now the acrid smell of shit came winging up as he crouched, beasted by a stranger now who fell for his erecting penis, fantasy-fed in the urinals of a favoured gay toilet and followed H, whose bait had hooked a monster that would not be easily assuaged by the little mouse. He followed, no words

exchanged, just Harry's thumping heart led the way
(the throb of fear not joy) to his room. And H
sacrificed himself to the idea that at some point
ecstasy would return and trade itself with this
ridiculous fear . . . and that as the stranger undid his
flies and fire started to ignite his loins, it would
continue and not abate . . . but the size of him! . . . it
was a threat . . . it was violent and would hurt . . . H
felt an unworthy combatant . . . felt small and puny.
The man was black and yes it was true . . . it was no
myth, since this one was indeed set like a
donkey . . . they do have vast quantities of cock . . .
and the small flame that lit a candle for H shrank
away as the guy, without asking, took some oil off
the shelf in the bathroom and poured it onto his
hands like a gladiator oiling himself for the battle to
the death . . . or as if a complex operation was about
to take place. He was priming his cock with a large
palmful of oil, too much, but of course with that
weapon how necessary! The black knew that his
shaft needed bountiful lubrication and whereas
a normal, hard and shrewd queen would have told
him with no qualms where to get off in an act of self-
preservation—what good is a stretched out
queen?—Harry could not. Harry was still shy in his
exploration into the realm of his sexual indentity.
The black had said nothing but sensed his alarm and
his fear . . . was even used to guys freaking out over
his tool and even turning on him, and he usually in
those cases ended up with a blow-job or a friendly
wank. He didn't mind which really, as long as he
released a binful of spunk with a whitey . . . as long as
he could be free in his body, and he sensed in Harry a
victim but read masochism in Harry's weakness
where he could have read simply fear . . . the black
was experienced and gave value to what he read in
men's faces when their voices were too shy to betray

their deepest longings ... in this case he was unaware that he was torturing H. How often do you come across a gay in his thirties who is still a virgin? As sex had removed itself from H it left a dry room where nothing could grow (the black senses the cold dry room deep within H and has no desire to enter that particular abode). H's sexual barometer remained flaccid ... and as the black squeezed and pummelled H's hanging appendage of skin, the emptiness of which drove the master even further into his quest for pain, he seemed determined to split poor H's intestines as an axe splits oak. How dare whitey not be 'hard on' with my beautiful black prick up his ass and half way up his stomach, his renewed vigour seemed to imply ... but H's hips ceased to move and just presented themselves to the black like some meagre sacrificial offering from a poor pagan to a demon deity, as if to say that's all we have ... it's not much, but it's living. *'Move, fuck you!! ... move onto my prick!!'* He seemed to shriek at H's dumb, prostrate white buttocks going gradually red with impatient kneading... Harry wobbled uneasily on his knees and wanted to collapse onto his stomach, but the black incensed now with the strength that lust loans to muscles (no matter how tired) to complete the act, held H up like a bag of flesh and bones with his right arm and pulled him onto the hilt where seemingly it could go no further... the black lifted his head and bared his teeth like a donkey about to bray, arched his back . . . said . . . 'OH FUCK FUCK FUCK OOOH SHIT YOU FUCKER (what pain) OOH FUUUCK YOU MOTHER YOU MOTHER FUCKING COCK-SUCKER...I'LL EAT YOU OOH MMMYY... LICK MY SPUNK...EAT MY SHIT OOOH OOOH NOOO WOW WOW WOWEE OH FUCK OH!! HONEY! NICE NICE HONEY? CHRIST-

OFUCK!' The black shuddered then fell down like a shot bull... panting over H's back... the weight of him collapsing finally H's precarious position... dead feelings crept into the proceedings... the world seemed to go very still and shadows would flit in and out of H's eyes as if bats or even vultures were in the room... waiting... numbness... did not even feel the shrinking of the black's penis as its spent swill having whooshed into H was now returning to the folds of peace... a death smell lingered, cold and dank around the prostrate limbs of the victim which seemed to impersonate the spread-eagled and twisted corpses of Auschwitz... sleep: H wanted sleep or to wrench himself free to throw himself out of the window... but most of all, what the sane part of his mind wanted, wanted more than anything else in the entire earth, was to cradle in his arms a soft gentle woman, a soft gentle and unfearful thing that had no pain... no threat... no hard muscle or rough bristle... no vile hot stabbing greed investing him with agony... no scummy dirt or breath-stink-shit-sour. Soft... soft... soft... the word comforted; talcum-powdered and tinkling voices ... soft faces... soft cheeks... soft bosoms and ribbons... innocent vulnerable thighs and always soft, soft, soft downy brown ... his ass felt cold and wet and even torn, as the organic compost of shit, sperm and blood dripped its unsightly mixture onto the sheets... He was sick and weak and was sure some time had passed; feeling a heavy weight on him, the sleeping black. So H had drifted off... had drifted off into a dream world peopled with the soft bodies, the sweet smelling bodies of women and woke to the shocking realisation of what the dead weight pinning him down was... and with it came the burning, like corrosive acid, from his anus and the awful memory of the *thing* that felt as if still there,

still undulating and thrusting and the black
screaming invectives, the chorus for his excited
secretions. Harry barely turned his head but could
just see out of the corner of his eye a large red patch
near his hips... his or mine? But more than likely
mine. He was circumcised and less likely to tear than
a man who hadn't been. H felt sick and tearful and
wanted the black growth like a burden from hell off
of his back and out... out for ever... but H could
only mutter . . . 'Please . . .Please . . . would you get
off me please . . . please . . . off me please . . . do you
hear?' *'Hello sweetheart...who's had a nappy
then... Hey! I must have had a shut eye... Ha! Ha!
Ha! nice one though, eh! Nice!'* As if the thought had
encouraged him and the ghastly sleep refreshed him,
H to his horror felt the man's slimy, sticky penis
reswelling itself for the act. No, the black couldn't
resume at this stage, must see how injured one of
them was. 'No . . . get off . . . please, I'm ill.' But if
fates worse than death had existed in H's
imagination this must answer for the supreme...
once again he penetrated... H attempted to twist
away, though still on his belly, not on his knees...
'Hold still cunt or I give it you!' ... he took Harry's
throat in his hands and gave a vicious but quick
squeeze, as if to say how simple it would be for my
powerful hands to snap this scrawny neck and how I
hate your scrawny neck and what it's attached to but
you must be obedient until I have had my fill... H
passed out for a second but had no doubt and read
well messages of violence! they need no analysis and
are not famous for inuendo. With his hands still
holding onto his throat the black moved, gyrating
like a dancer into the wound of the world... Harry's
poor torn sphincter... he moved like he had all the
time he needed and could indulge and savour as a

gourmet whose first fierce hunger having been
appeased, is able to relax and enjoy rather than
satisfy . . . 'please, please don't'. . . a pathetic whine
gurgled from his bloody mouth . . . wherefore doth
blood come into his mouth!!! Did he bite his tongue
or did his heart burst!! The black heaved with a more
spikey vigour . . . *'On your knees . . . Oh come on
turd . . . I'm nearly there . . . Shit I nearly . . . Nearly . . . Come on . . . I can't like this . . . On your knees
you fucker . . . Come on mother . . . Thaaats better . . . Heeeeah . . . Oh wow . . . Hey thats wuuunder-
ful . . . Oh . . . Oh . . . Ohh!!!!! Ow Woow!'* The negro
still held Harry by the throat and H was impaled to
the hilt . . . he was thrusting hard now and arched his
back once more and as his moment of triumph came,
bared his teeth, as if to holler it to the whole
world . . . did not of course see the blood seeping out
of Harry's mouth nor feel the slackness when death
calmly extinguishes the lights of a body . . . OOW . . .
OW . . . OW . . . OW . . . OW . . . OW . . . OW . . .
OW . . . OH YEAH!!!!! YEAH!!!! OOOOO-
OOOOH!

False God

Alone in the room... all alone and silent with nothing and no one... his sex locked away in a vault bound with manacles of fear... rusting and petrifying into the cold iron... alone... feeling only a warm drowsiness induced by the spluttering gas fire... cold on the inside warm on the outside... growing older by the minute... The strands of taut life slackening... a life that had thrust him through a thousand orifices... hard as a chain that drives a machine, oiled and lubricated, the force of his drive was once as strong as a new 2 stroke engine, his thrust was as rapid, and his viscous explosions were once an unending source of pleasure to the thousand or so women he estimated he had splattered his silken jets into... A seemingly limitless supply, a cornucopia of spunk seemed to be his mass of flesh, unending until death, a perennial bloom, with each valve and tissue, vein and artery conjoining in a holy alliance to produce in his sacks the vital DNA. The Sting... the magic paste to weld life together, cell by molecular cell sewn by a host of minute fairies. He would aim his swollen tool into warm, pulsating, rubbery caves whose owners squealed at the new tenant's occupation of their many and multifarious rooms. He had wanted to populate the world... to cram into those blind and to him, screaming hungry mouths, his generous flesh, to be an unending supply to an unending demand, to satisfy and fulfil the hunger of the female human race ... his ambition had been thus fuelled by such motives ... as if nothing else in life that he had seen or felt capable of was worth achieving, since it was all so vapid and ephemeral. No career could compensate for the time it stole from your youth; for the time it snatched from the need and act of love ... and it not only stole time but sapped the flower and drained the perfume, as some youth with bent spine hung his head into musty tomes resembling nothing more than a wilting daffodil ... these intellectual eunuchs with their seldom exercised shafts of cocooned flesh ... only books they produced or symphonies to amuse the masses or to distract them from their own need to be fulfilled ... nodding their heads in some vast sterile palace of culture to the frenzied baton of a geriatric whilst their brains were swarming with distracted dreams of lubric pleasures. The vagina and penis would create their own symphonic variations ... knew for certain that his baton could excite more than anything else in the world's treasure house of sensations ... No woman could be possessed by anything more powerful and amazing than a sizeable hunk of mankind stirring up between her thighs a froth of gore-dew whilst disturbing their minds with sexual dramas as intense as Shakespeare's Sonnets. So, his ascent into the world of sex had been swift and prodigious, had taken all he could and gave always more. He had drained himself like a river until the sediments and rocks were exposed, yet he would be refilled again as if by the omnipotent ocean ... filled ... blown up with a riot of blood called by the brain into action. And they truly loved him for it ... he gave to many and refused none ... was a Jesus dividing his loaf among

the multitudes and the more he gave the greater
seemed his capacity. Everyone had their fill and few
complained although some demanded of him the
sacrifice of totality to themselves ... that he break
his rock only into them, had not understood his
mission which was to all, a calling from the Most
High who had instilled in him this God-like
capacity. They had been gently dealt with though
sometimes furious scenes ensued as if the sacrifice of
their bellies demanded the life-long enchaining of
the beast that fed them. But this animal must hunt
like the lion and the wolf and no one enchains
them ... must have many litters and enlarge the scope
of nature since God, Pan or Zeus had created him
for this role ... his sap must feed mankind and create
much fruit ... a rich harvest lay in his rotund balls
and as she guides his prick into her belly his eyes
closed with the familiar feeling of home and on
opening them gazed on the many different
expressions on their faces ... as he ground his pestle
into their mortar, undulating it as if to explore every
corner of a new continent, their faces would take on
the expressions of Greek tragic masks, so caught
were the features into themselves. They might look
pained but were concentrating on catching the
visions that soar up like multi-coloured Birds of
Paradise disturbed from their sleep in the dense
foliage ... swam in oceans of sensations as his stack
chocked them and for others it dislodged the dust
from the walls and broke the crust of neglect and
light poured into their wombs as into a long
neglected tomb and they came to life again as their
lips wept hot unguents and a myriad of tremors
shook their continents and rivers swelled their banks
and fish poured upstream to lay their eggs and then
he would leave, withdraw only after a long and
supreme effort ... when his exploration had exposed

every part that was capable of exploration. Constant fucking removed the fear of premature ejaculation and whilst he would enjoy it more and savour and relish the delights his gates to the dam would remain obdurately closed... until the right moment when she would come, dissolve and flow downstream, after the rages of the falls and rapids had tossed her into madness... The peaceful aftermath when floating gently in her own liquids ... he'd unleash his quiet load of spunk... note the prick jerk and rear its head, pulse out its last exclamations and be still... a dead thing, slain. To come before her would be anathema to him, would pull him back to the earth before he left the gravitational field, would plummet him down to be impaled upon a savage cliff, helpless like Prometheus, blown by icy winds... not melting in a volcano that he had made erupt or hurtling to the stars, but impotent and marooned, scummed by his own seed... but thought he, 'Good'... another target, another sacrifice to his altar where the pudenda was worshipped as the cradle of life... not lifeless stone or remote deity, or preaching celibate or ghostly historical ascetic or dead words in cracked and dusty books, but alive... there... now... he worshipped the Mary of her cunt. All cunt was holy and all screamed aloud for blessing... his duty and his prayers were to the filling and blessing of it... cunt is the Temple of God and is the cradle of life and God fills the orifice with his presence and enters his prick too since the God Head is a twin deity... and no cunt is ever different from another cunt except as a face is different, since at the moment that the Almighty enters and illuminates his altar he shows his face to be there, smiling with the savage grin of a satyr... but God will only enter the cunt at that moment when it becomes alive and flowers and is filled, for only then will He give his blessing. Thus am I a religious being, a devout priest ... a holy Man of God ... his saint on earth and verily do I worship at God's chosen temples within whose walls I offer myself up to him ... 'Hear Oh Ye Kings, Give Ear Oh Ye Princes, I, Even I Will Sing Unto the Lord' ... and people came from far and wide to genuflect at his altar of Priapus and his benificent, swollen-cheeked, roseate God winked down at his High Priest's devotion and blessed his flesh and urged it on to greater and greater feats and fine webs of skin were formed in countless soft caves catching and weaving miracles of the aftermath that he set in motion ... Some alas did not bear fruit and some were viciously cast out into the night by violent hands in brilliantly lit chambers of horror, where gleamed sharp and relentless scalpels in whose reflection moved convex shapes in white, like stealthy murdering ghosts ... these others did not want the host planted there since many liked only the digging and the rooting, therefore much sinew and fine membrane became a feast for the sewer rats or was burned at terrible sacrifices ... and these events caused in him terrible pangs of guilt and sleepless nights when he would suddenly awake, alone and through custom, forgetting for the moment that he was alone and unsuccessful that day, turn over to grasp for comfort the warm woman that was usually there ... but she wasn't and he'd clasp his own empty space and knot his grey sheets in his fists and moan into his seamy pillow and bewail that dozens of women were alone too, many hundreds and yet here he was ... alone, and the thought of them lying likewise alone and needing him plunged him into even greater confusion ... or else they were with other men ... others were clasping the flesh he so much needed now ... others were grinding their hips and tying their tongues into wet knots . . . and she was admiring some man and being bathed in the seat of his effort but not him! . . . And she was opening her eyes in wonder as the man was stabbing her groin with his vile sceptre, and screaming as she came, but not for him that sweet sound . . . and from all over the city he imagined the wails of fornication issuing from the mouths of thousands upon thousands, and the rivers of spunk that must be flowing that night or any night but not his, and imagined the moaning of their voices rising in unison like sirens to torment him and strained his ears and seemed to catch the sound floating on the wind . . . And the thought burned into his temples and he mourned as for a dead one, wailed why she wasn't here . . . any she, since they are all the same . . . all of them . . . different only in the size of shoes or taste in music or degree of sugar in their coffee and yes they liked to think each one was so different to the other, so unique, so special, unlike any other creature in the world but when God entered their bodies they became HIM . . . God-struck . . . 'and I am faithful only to him whose presence in the flesh I communicate with . . . I fuck for God's sake!' But wasn't God manifested in other flesh, those others that were entwined like honey-suckle twisting in and out of the dark sleeping streets and shuttered windows, whilst he lay empty and aching. Was he not there in the bodies of others that performed as he did? But he could not conceive that He was there in the true spirit as He is in me . . . in me exists the world . . . outside me lives nothing . . . outside of me nothing exists but for the fact that I perceive it in my own mind . . . in my mind exists the universe . . . cut out my mind and it ceases to be. Therefore God can exist only for me. I cannot feel my cock in some other man's cock or feel her cunt being stabbed by him ... I can only know it, and knowing it hurts ... Then in torments of anguish did he fitfully sleep in a bed, slimy and unkempt... in a room with a stove to one side and some half-eaten, take-away chop suey that was congealing in a paper carton on the sideboard... An ash-tray filled with butt-ends like dead locusts and a sink next to the stove filled with dirty week-old crockery. And he grew worse as his desperation to worship God increased and in increasing, the intensity of his search frightened off those whom the Gods themselves imbue with their spirit and they sought new altars. One Winter H surveyed his dim eye in the glass and with his finger-tips adjusted his receding greying hair, turned on the gas fire and so felt warm again. He sat in the chair feeling drowsy but not wracked by walking the streets and searching cafés for the lonely that he'd try to induce to his now threadbare feast... God, thought H was deserting him now and even his limp flesh felt stringy as though by no power could this flaccid thing ever be metamorphosed into the instrument it once had been. God has deserted me... Or else did I worship false Gods?... No... Perhaps, H mused, it was a punishment... a chastisement for the lives of the innocent and unborn that were sent back to him unclaimed... Thereafter, when many moons had driven the seed of life through millions of women and Autumn had once again paraded past his windows flecked in the riotous colours of nature dazzled by its own life force, he decided that what he needed to fulfil God's wishes was a wife... To share the seasons and witness the glow of life illume her each month and bear the fruit of his seed and feel the ebbs and flows of her tides. In this way would he make amends and expiate any sin he might have unconciously committed in his zealous worshipping.

He would worship God anew, and so he looked, and no one looked more fiercely or committed themselves with such ardour, but somehow he felt that time was out of joint for him and even the approaching of a female was now so painful in anticipation of rejection that his courage would fail. He prayed to God but his prayers were evidently not heard and he remained alone in his room with the gas fire. But as chance will have it what is suited to you will sense your need or you will eventually sense it, and be led to your goal. So he found himself one day, just as Spring was beginning to nudge the merest swelling in the buds and the cherry blossoms were sending dizzy eyed creatures silly with joy, found himself in a seedy area of the city near the commercial section, having finished his shift as a night porter in a third class hotel... there, in a shop window was a sight that caught his eye and fuelled his imagination and not without some pangs of lust. She was pretty... nay even beautiful, and stared back at him with that ever-so-slightly haughty glance that interested women adopt as if to veil their true inclination. He went inside the shop... The first time that he ever dreamed of going into one of those places having hitherto no need of them, and very quietly asked the assistant who was a rather sympathetic lady how much it was... and pointed since he could not frame the words, to the inflatable woman in the window... After, and in the confines of his room he found that although she wasn't his ideal she nevertheless was extremely sweet and was indeed built such as the manufacturers guaranteed... It was quite incredible and when a shiver of life re-ignited his member with the current that had for so long been absent he climbed aboard the plastic replica and wept to God for at last forgiving him and worshipped him at his new shrine... holding his wife in his arms he poured sweet nothings into her ear and swore eternal devotion...she smiled mysteriously and numbly back.

North

DAY ONE

Got on my bike—Homer and Ulysses beckon whenever I am kissed and licked by the sun. Drove to the end of the road, seas hard and painful bright blue. Clouds are dappled grey, sinews creep out darkening the sea—seaweed in long tapering fingers in the shallow emerald green. Sky fresh now as washed linen, clouds, puffy mashed potato, fields thick with rolling spinach, cascading down like liquid velvet or paint, or paint running and smudging—streaked! A bramble, a tree trunk hits the eye as the eye-radar swirls and scans around the skull. Stop the bike, it steams like a marathon runner; walk, spreading thicket; God, foot in stream, in rut, in swamp, in marsh, squelch and onwards. Me, chest hard, heaving, breathing, smelling the odour of ordure, a slush of fresh baked dung newly—damn!—broken by my blind foot; misplaced, the dung is fresh again, shiny. Wool on wire—wind stops, and for a second the world hangs silent. Eyes scan into the distant receding vista witnessing there in the middle of my vision a sail cutting the loch, two birds swoop on something— looking like hawks as they do, silhouette black against the sky they cut a piece out and wheel out of

107

sight. Up, spore marks in the sky, whispered secrets, white moustaches. Then the wind blows that sound again, really a sighing of mourners in a large echoing Cathedral at Cologne. Breath snatched from the trees, air, sea, loch. Its taste is stored and expelled, big shadows on the hills move slowly, you know, like stains, sweat stains which move—dark patches. The sheep scatter in quick steps at your approach. Sun high and cold, gleaming with snatches of windless heat. The loch and hills fade into the disappearing apex of your vision as a primitive timeless landscape. Your bike gleams and cools and waits. It moves you more easily than you move yourself. You sit and it moves, you turn a handle and it thrusts immediately between your legs, shivers, and bundles of power and cool air refreshes. It waits, your steel servant, steel and spoked rubber. For now you would rather be under the sun-baked heather dung-stung air, sea-choked and weed-filtered peat of centuries, than your machine. A beetle hurtles to the underworld in a peaty stream trapped into stagnancy by a receding tide. With some weed, and blocking his entrance, the beetle dives and wiggles aimlessly and then comes up for air in little wiggly jerky movements. The loch turns to the blue of outer-space pure where it deepens into cerulean and violet. Dusk, the stars are thrown across the sky as if handfuls of seed fixed into the black, cold, sharp needle-points staring down at the scene, star-tracks scorch home through the ether burning nocturnal emission; a sliver of white, a luminous bow, Cupid's Arrow, a bit of dust, 'Oh look, a shooting star!' It disappears as fast.

Sleep.

DAY TWO

The sun scorches on the neck, the boats are frozen in a lake of tears; memory waves beckon and soften the determination of the spine. A sparrow hovers over a spider in a clump of grass, fluttering in space not moving only airborne, wing-tips, neck bent down resembling an upturned trembling hook.

I saw swans in the lake that was still as a mirror, throwing the sky's face back. The swans idled out as alabaster carvings. The breakfast was nice, the tea drained through the plumbing and squashed and mashed the eggs. Slept fitfully, tossing and turning, trying to find the right cipher in my bed, the right symbol that would bring peace to my twisted body, curled, stretched. Oh for sleep, oh the rage in the guts. The laughter from the other rooms, let me get drunk oh Lord, let me thrive in the wreckless abandonment of my senses, let me career aimlessly and thoughtless with outsize voice and slither through emotional visceral lakes where dams have been broken, and it all gets mixed up. Let me touch on madness and giggle furiously in the ridiculous quivering spectacle of myself turning into a mass of wobbling joy. Oh the control, let me let it go, let me be free—to sing and scream and howl, reaching down into my stomach with trowels and bull-dozers to smash and excavate the hardened and constipated life stuck to the walls, burn it off, shudder and explode into life.

DAY THREE

Breathless I was—aghast! Gulping for air, steadfast on my machine, I was hurled 200 miles, stopping to refuel in the awful main road tourist route, the ghastly coaches lined with waxed portraits staring out of stale bodies (or rather containers). Oh, oh, oh my God ... The hills move as I zip through them. They curl around me and wave and slip a few valleys in, gorges and passes (yes). Or rise higher and higher and slither down in loose rock sediment chippings and silt, and sometimes the hills astride, I hurtle through them; they wait for me, inviting you to skim through the centre, what's on the horizon? Unravelled mantles of ochre and sea-green, and up spun a dove and then a starling swept across me. A swift, a swallow. Did it dive down—did it disappear—tears in the wind-gripped eyes—the wild wind-swept 80 mph, and choked blast cut and slashed, cold fingers of ice play softly on your face. Oh the sun aches and twists, bulges, and seems ready to burst. Oh it changes colour now, tries on a gown or 'whose party, darling will this do?' Black thin trees splatter the space and cut, tattoo themselves over the sun's belly. She looks well tonight—it heaves itself out of the forest dragging tangles of branches; it's dark, it vomited out of the mountain like the birth of Apollo, trailing nerve endings it hides and the cool dull wind, sad wind, chastens and it's lonely without the warm-hearted red rotund bursting cherry-big scorched friend who hides, oh she peeks out now, sends long piercing stalks of light out; she's there. Tin lines—lines of tin crushed auto-spectators move in a line down the road. Four bikes overtake me; bikes overtaking undoubtedly wave. Facing opposite directions, zoning towards each other at combined speeds of 160 mph they will usually, not always, but usually flash their front-light, but in passing may wave. These do, the long line of tin cars is oppressive, they move like a sick and dying caterpillar crawling for a space to expire. The other cars, now a longer space. Is there room ahead, flash

frequent but frequent enough—not to risk overtaking. A narrow road, you see, full of bends! Quite
a few hills, no direct view for 75 yards so you
overtake quickly and suddenly if you see just a bit of
space then are swallowed back into the stream
allowing the on-coming cars their space, since they
bring towards you, in the opposite direction, a half
ton of power fast enough to hurl you into vertical
ascent if you do not side-step quickly enough. There
are blind bends, blind hills, blind but carrying a
certain sense of death. You join the tin necklace, are
you the jewel in between? They lie sunken in their
seats in front, you imagine the chat, the kiddies
climb over the seat. Some artificial thing, revolting,
waves its head, sitting in the back-rest, it waves its
head like an insane creature on the back-seat, it
waves its head with red eyes. Clouds gather at the
corner of the frame and the wind reverses into your
chest; flies meet your goggles with squelchy
embraces, a little farmhouse—shall we live there
dear? Grinding out corn and wheat—baking our
own bread. Where dear? It's gone. It's now a waterfall. Where dear? It's gone. It's now a field. Where?
It's gone—it's gone—a horse, a clump of trees, an
empty space, a streak of green, zoom! zoom! two
cars, now a longer space. Is there room ahead, flash
on my winker, right hand, and open up the throttle.
It starts, it easily overtakes. Good, there's space
ahead, enough in case another car in front has pulled
out too, so safe if not for him for me, but no—he
pulls sharply, returns to the womb from whence he
came. He returns, just sneaking back into the space
he left and leaving me to face, in the distance, that
from which he withdrew. At the speed of light, the
opponent's lights snap on, warning me he can go
nowhere. On his left a steep incline, behind others
hurtling too fast for sudden decision—so hell, I pull

out all my stops to overtake, just one small metal cylinder of flesh packed with sweat, pock-marked, fag-choked. I have just 50 yards at least but oh why doesn't it overtake? I stay the same; ahead he's blinking at me. 25 yards, why my bike will not sweep up and overtake; the monster on my left with grin and piss-off chortle speeding out to stop me, will not drop back—prevents my returning to the fold. He's increased his speed to keep me on the right lane. I drop behind but my space is taken by another; he's alarm-filled, quick I turn and see his panic. He's moved up but behind him others have moved up too—the lump of screaming tin still speeds forbidding me to overtake. I scrape so close to him we might be twins, the scum and filthy seated piece of human flesh afraid now in case I come too close, breaks now to let me in. Oh God, too late, too late . . . The roaring ton ahead with open maw is on me, eyes turn to water, heart to milk, it's there, it grows . . . scream.

ONE SECOND LATER

With the ripening corn, small and shiny black things wriggle under the sun and spinners plait and weave under brambles overgrown for the season. Cloudless now, blue hot scorched tight moodless stretched sheet of sky so fine and the earth has been scraped and the peat, funnelled and turned for small trees growing—pines—forests will come. The giant eagles claw the skies at Ardnamurchan in Ballachulish— the sun throws millions of lights into the Loch and the dead sleep in the churchyard peacefully. Somewhere from above a deluge of rain—in red? Imagine it slowly and dreamily, like an ice-flow breaking up in the Spring solstice. The screeching—

the screaming of brakes, hand and foot squeezing,
pushing down, passenger ahead flying through dash-
board window as if diving into pools on razor-clear
August mornings. The glass shimmers and dissolves
on impact like splashing water—mixed with (the passenger this) a detached vein here—by itself, located
in the neck—unhooked from home by a clever sliver
of glass left from a mid-air split-second-time,
stopped-shutter-frozen leap—then continue, the
vein moving like an agitated worm searching—blind
worm being born alive by the power of the flow that
cascades freely out, the oil tank that cracked and
dripping—rent body of the car from the gross
intrusion (how dare you) of another car up its rear
end—piercing and foully penetrating—oiled and
splutter—shatter. Body of one, the swallow-diver on
the tarmac—fountain still on—the driver biting on
the wheel—his teeth, sprung out or buried bits in
lips, redistributed you might say. But in any case
saved by the wheel which only cracked a rib or two,
nudging the curved bone of his ribs into the lung—
only (oh go on!). But the petrol—oil and blood mix
(not well) on the tarmac. It's hot now we've stopped,
so hot the bike—mine—had simply annihilated
itself. Its front became a ragout of rubber, spokes
and steel and separated from the rest, as if it had
been shaved off—close! The rest just melted (as if)
and twisted by an angry mighty fist... and you
'describe what you saw,' I saw the sky rise up and the
earth recede below. I travelled high above the vile
throng as if thrown and witnessed a lake I had not
seen before from the ground but up it shone as bright
as silver from my vantage point in space, as bright as
a dollar, and small figures were gathered at its edge
with fishing rods, standing very still and calm, and
still the valley moved across my eyes. A plane
murmured high, leaving a thin small mark in the

impervious blue and from below I witnessed the snake had stopped, bunching up into its centre and then finally quiet. At the point of impact dense segments growing wider towards the tail and the faces staring out red; this one with blotch and tape over the nose, face out, hand over mouth like this, straining to see, breast heaving in a marzipan orange low-cut Marks and Sparks sweater with kiddie-winks crawling over. 'Get down Richard.' 'Oh let me see mum!' Whacks and looks, eyes grovelling and hungry for bits of flesh that should be attached, horror-hungry. 'Oh did you'—she says, blonde short-bobbed hair, large teeth, voice a gurgle with orgasmic excitement, throat opened and released—'did you . . . see it? Ooooooh it was—he just—that car!! It was ooooooh!' Sibilant and gleaming teeth with piece of gum stacked in the corner of the mouth for future use. The scene slowly moves but imperceptively, not that you'd notice really—flying in space, the azure deepening to purple, the trees racing together—melting as one; the river turned to a thin line or scar or spit-gleam tracing its way into the distance and the loch to a half-dollar piece, the tin snake is still in heat-sweat—the kids are crying and the road is smeared with its compost of oil, blood and the shit that flew out of the combatants. Glass and wire of human and machine entangle. Burn.

TWO MINUTES LATER

I was hurled amongst the stars, thrown by an almighty power and tossed into the deep of painless space, vacuumed into oblivion and into velvet layers I entrust myself. My body's turned to ash, my skin to molecules, my eyes to atoms, my blood to neutrons;

then spun into space my disembodied atoms
resemble a galaxy—a universe of stars—I spread as I
travel speed of light years ahead. The atoms drift
apart leaving so much space between each one, but
not lost. From the edge of the universe, from there, I
still resemble—still look like me but close to I'm just
a mass of space and emptiness but the thoughts are
whistling transmogrified into energy and waves
lassoing the universe, lassoing the planet. Earth
hallo, can you hear me? They're waking up in San
Francisco, to bed in Shoreditch. Later. Where is he?
she wonders, throwing the cat out and bolting the
door. He's late. Late? (Bone splintered, eyes burst
open by shock.) She puts the milk-bottle out (an arm
is severed, lying in a field of corn; she loved that arm
stroking her so finely). She turns on the reading
light, looked forward to him strong and young in his
years, he strides over them not weighed down—
where's the sound of his bike, he should be back by
now. Her ears alert, tentacles taut, eyes wide for
every bike that comes down the street, but
recognising the chortle throb. No, not that one, no
not that, where is he now, he's late. Dinner-heating,
cat scratching at window (invisible angels flutter
over the sight of hell with puckered mouths, hands
clasped to head like old rabbis, gestures of shrug and
is there any hope?) 'Did you see it?' Slowly. 'Be a
witness.' Whilst he flies into the third circle of the
universe, the world now is spirit-lamp lit one side.
She's gone to bed. Oh come on, cuddle and stroke
and I'll put my knees behind you like chairs. His wife
is soft—your limbs are dismembered. Imagine
yourself with her, the ticking of the clock, your hand
on her hip, resting gently as if... only hear her
breathing. Don't place yourself there now—
unstitched skin is horrible, disorganised, not nice.

A caterpillar slides over a leaf, buckling up and crawling out again, head in the air twitching like a metronome, undecided, settles eventually to nibble on the edge of the leaf, mandibles working furiously, the leaf disappears slowly resembling a sieve—now what does it think as its shining black head pours over its salad? Back to the scene. Oh he's hurt, the one with the plaster nose-protector uttered, don't look Ethel—grunts fat and sloppy with a battered hat, don't look for God's sake, there's tiny dew-drops of blood on the window-screen and we're six cars back—ugh! Get a cloth, wipe the windscreen for Christ's sake, it's dry Bert, it's dry, it just makes a smear! Ohhh! All that was inside him and now it's on the wind-shield. Your husband is on the wind-shield. Just wipe it off Ethel! Wipe me off—what constitutes me? My blood—my organised body, broken, am I still me? But it's dry! So spit on it Ethel, do it—oh for fucks sake! You do it! Don't say that in front of the—fuck it, just give it to me, I'll do it. A spiral of sanguine red spun out under the sun, sprayed the crops, anointed the road, slimed the cars, freckled the windows, dyed his clothes, fed the flies, and he was in the blood as the blood was in him before he took off for other worlds. But blood held the passion together, pasted the thoughts and fed the motor, drove the piston and filled his organ for acts of riot and spell and magic at carnivals of flesh where now no more will he create the future world, now it lay defeated as a thousand dreams and anguished moans lay shattered with it. Witness the pretty faces flying out of his mind as he leaves this world—see his life flying past him with small soft faces embedded as jewels in a bracelet of his thought, or raisins in a cake—childlike faces fringed with tassles of downy hair. Choose one. The rain starts to fall. He'll be wet.

He'll come in soaking and cold with his knees and thighs drenched through; the afternoon was so hot the cat slept in the shadow of the dustbin. His cottage-cheese in the fridge, a light is on in the hall. A salad sits greenly in a bowl, dressing in a little cup. There is a nice new silky nightie, an old Victorian slinky silky nightie that holds my body in its warmth, as if it were holding something precious. The tick of the gas-meter breaks the silence. Is there a key in the lock? He's come, foot-steps perhaps? The world turned yellow, red, then a whitish blue and I joined a swarm like bees or atoms like a cloud of locusts, and we, this cloud and me, moved together, each particle attracting the other, each neutron circling around in its own energy-filled and they held me within them and feeling no fear I soared and was happy to be part of this radiant universe, and colours fractured and melted, changed and prismatised, violet sunk into vermillion and became scorched magenta. Worlds drifted past in smelting gaseous glows which always looked so solid.

The world's most experienced airline.